THE SEA CAPTAIN'S
ORPHANED DAUGHTER

ELLA CORNISH

CHAPTER 1

*T*illy Wainwright raced through the house, her satin slippers sliding this way and that on the newly polished wooden floor as she did so. Normally she would laugh and giggle at how it felt, as if she was skating on an icy winter pond, but today was an incredibly special day and there was nothing on her mind but the fact that her father was coming home after several months away at sea.

"Matilda!" her aunt Ruth called out as she flew past the sitting room. "Do slow down before you fall and hurt yourself. That would never do on the day of your father's return. Now, would it?"

"I simply can't!" she called out, the crimson satin ribbons of her pretty dress fluttering in her wake.

She had put her special dress on for this momentous occasion, wanting to look her very best for her darling papa's return. After all, it had been four long months since she had last seen him and every time he returned home he always brought something special for her. Last time he had presented her with a large seashell with a carving of a tropical island on it. It had pride of place on her bedside drawers and every morning she would look at it longingly, waiting for her father to return home.

Tilly reached the hallway and peered out of the window by the front door, her brow crumpling as she did so. It was a cloudless day, with no rain falling— not like it had been for the past week, keeping her indoors with her aunt, learning her letters and numbers. At the age of eight, Tilly was way beyond where she should be for someone of her age. She found the work too easy and boring. Before long, her aunt would have difficulty in challenging Tilly's mind.

She also detested what her Aunt Ruth thought she should be doing, such as practicing her embroidery or finishing her sampler.

Now that her father was to be home soon, however, Tilly knew that there would be late night stories of the places that he had visited, and she would be snuggled against his big, burly chest, hearing the rhythm of his heart and breathing in the faint scent of tobacco and the briny sea air that always clung to him.

They would play games and he would let her stay up past her bedtime, no matter how much Aunt Ruth scolded him.

Tilly couldn't wait for her father to come home.

She didn't know how long she had been standing in the hallway, anxiously watching every figure as they passed by, feeling more and more disappointed when it wasn't her dear papa.

Then, as it was nearing mid-morning, she saw him, and her heart squeezed with joy as she hurried to the front door. "Matilda Wainwright, do not open that door!" her aunt stated firmly, her hands firmly on her hips. "Now, you are going to greet your Papa properly, like a young lady should, or I will not let you have dessert tonight."

Tilly stuck out her lip. Tonight, cook would make her father's favourite dessert, bread and butter pudding with a good helping of raspberry jam. Her mouth began watering at the very thought. Since it was his favourite, it was hers too.

So, she didn't open the door, clasping her hands together so tightly that they hurt as she waited for her father to push it open.

"I know you are excited," her aunt said as she touched Tilly's shoulder lightly. "But let's show your Papa that you haven't forgotten your manners in his absence."

"Yes," Tilly answered, watching the doorknob for any sign of movement. She just wanted to see her father.

When the doorknob did finally rattle, Tilly held her breath, her heart thudding in anticipation.

He was finally here.

Then his large body filled the doorway and she let out an excited cry, rushing towards him, not caring about her manners at all. "Papa!"

He chuckled as he caught her and swung her around in his arms, his thick woollen coat smelling of the sea. "Is that my darling daughter? It simply can't be, why last time I saw her she was half the size!"

Tilly squealed as the room spun, throwing her arms around his broad neck. "Oh, I've missed you, Papa!"

"And I've missed you, my sweet," he stated, his rough beard tickling her cheek. Tilly didn't mind it one bit, instead breathing in his familiar scent. Suddenly the house seemed a whole lot warmer with him home, and her heart was bursting with happiness.

Finally, he lowered her to the floor, his eyes looking over her head. "Ruthie, it's good to see you, too."

"Hello, George," Aunt Ruth sniffed, crossing her arms over her chest. "It took you long enough this time."

Tilly watched as her father drew up to his full height, his smile broadening. "One would think that you missed me as well."

"Your charm doesn't work on me," she reminded him, dropping her arms. "I will go see about lunch. I'm sure you are famished after your journey."

They watched her walk down the hallway before Tilly turned back to her father. He had dropped his bag on the floor, and she stared at it curiously. "What did you bring me this time, Papa?"

His eyes twinkled. "What makes you think I brought you anything at all, Tilly?"

Tilly placed her hands on her slim hips, wrinkling her nose. "Because you always do, of course!"

Captain George Wainwright looked down at his daughter, the perfect likeness of his dear departed wife, Gracie, whom he missed something fierce every day. There wasn't a day that went by when he didn't think of his wife and how she had given up her own life to bring their beloved daughter into this world. Tilly was the only reason he ever came home from the sea. "You're right," he answered softly, tickling her under her chin. "But this time, I brought *us* something."

Tilly's eyes widened. "What did you bring?"

He reached down and opened the mouth of his bag, pushing aside the clothes that were crumpled inside before finding the flat board that he had carefully tucked away so that it wouldn't get broken. It had cost him a pretty farthing, that was for sure, but once he had seen it, he knew that he had to have it.

"What is it?" his daughter asked as he handed the object to her.

"Open it and see," he answered, reaching for the small canvas bag that held the remainder of the present.

Tilly looked down at the thin twine that held the brown paper together, almost not wanting to open the present. Once she did, the excitement would be over with.

"Go on," her father stated, holding a small canvas bag in his large hand, "it's not like you to dawdle, Tilly."

Tilly obediently did as he asked, frowning as she stared at the checkered wooden square in her hands. "I don't understand."

"It is a chess board," her father said, excitement in his voice. "It is a very popular game at the moment."

Tilly swallowed her displeasure. "But I don't know how to play."

"Not to worry, I'm going to teach you. With your abilities, you're bound to catch on soon enough," her father answered, reaching into the small canvas bag. "Look at these amazing pieces, Tilly, my girl. Only the best for us."

In his hand he held what amounted to be little more than a pile of wooden carvings, but Tilly conjured up a faint smile. Her father was home. That was all that mattered really.

Her father took the board from her and picked up his bag. "We will start your lessons after dinner this evening."

After dinner, as promised, Tilly followed her father into his study. "Let's sit by the fire," he said, rubbing his hands together gleefully.

Tilly noted the board set up on the small table between the two blue wingback chairs and wished that he would have brought her something different, such as a new story book that they could read together or another game, other than chess. "Papa, I want to hear about your travels tonight."

Her father waved a hand at her. "Later, Tilly, my girl. I want to teach you this game and it's going to take more than one lesson in order for you to catch on. Why, your own Papa played with the Admiral when we last docked at port! Of course, I had to let him win and not upstage him, but he even shook my hand and told me that I had been a well-matched partner for him." He met her eyes. "That is what I want for you, Tilly, my girl."

"Yes, Papa," Tilly said automatically, not wanting to upset him. If the game meant that much to him, then she would learn it and learn it well.

The captain ruffled her pretty dark curls fondly before moving to the sideboard. "That's my girl. Let me get myself something to drink and we will begin the lesson."

IT WAS the first hint of spring when her father came home from the sea, for good. "Good for nothing miscreants!" he yelled, pacing the sitting room floor where Tilly and Aunt Ruth had been seated quietly, going through Tilly's learning. This time there were no warm hugs, no presents or fond greetings. Tilly hadn't even known that her father was due to return so soon, and it had been quite a shock to see him in the hallway during the morning.

"Calm down, George," her aunt said in a hushed whisper as she clenched her hands in her lap tightly. "Can't you see you're scaring your child."

Her father let out a harsh laugh and stopped his pacing. "Scaring her? Scaring her! She should be frightened! Everything, every farthing I have left, is in my pocket! They didn't even bother to wish me well!"

Tilly swallowed hard as she observed her father's puce face. Something wasn't right, she had never seen him this angry before.

"It is not the end of everything," Aunt Ruth stated. "Surely, you can find a position in town."

"I was a sea captain, Ruth!" he bellowed, pulling at his wild hair. "A captain and they have thrown me over for some ruddy young buck that probably can't tell the hull from the mast! I gave them twenty years of my life! Twenty years, do you hear me! Then they turf me out over one little indiscretion, one that no one would have known about if it hadn't been for that young buck tittle-tattling."

Her aunt huffed as Tilly sank deeper into the chair, not liking the sound of her father's tone or his coarse words. Was he not a captain any longer? She had loved to hear his stories of his seafaring adventures, to smell the sea on him and hope that one day, when she was of age, that he would take her with him so she could see some of those faraway places as well.

"Well, I'm not going to sit here and listen to you yell and blaspheme," her aunt finally said, rising from her chair. She beckoned for Tilly to do the same and as much as Tilly wanted to stay with her father, she didn't like to hear him shout so loudly. "Perhaps you could calm down and then we can talk about this in a manner that will be productive. Come along, Tilly. Let's continue your lessons in another room."

Tilly bit her lip as she followed behind her aunt, not daring to glance back at her father. All was going to be well. Her father wouldn't let them be put out on the streets, would he?

She left him alone for four days as he closeted himself in his study, drinking himself into a stupor. When she eventually entered the room, she found him slumped in the chair before the fireplace, staring at it blankly. "Papa?" she asked hesitantly. "Would you like to teach me some more about chess?" She had found herself enjoying his lessons, their time together, but had yet to defeat him, which would have meant her lessons were coming to an end.

He gave her a faint smile, his eyes rimmed-red. "Ah, Tilly, my girl, I don't feel much like playing at the moment."

"Please, Papa," she begged, settling in the chair across from him. "Perhaps it will take your mind off your worries for a while."

He looked at her for a moment before letting out a heavy sigh and sitting up, wiping a weary hand over his face. "Perhaps it will, Tilly. Perhaps it will."

Tilly obediently sat straighter, reaching for the first piece. She would play her best and perhaps her father would give her a smile again.

Over the next few weeks, Tilly encouraged her father to play more often, so much so that she started to choose better moves, surprising him, beyond belief. "That's good, Tilly, my girl," he stated, his eyes becoming a little clearer than they had been. "Look how you have given me naught but one move that will be to your advantage."

Tilly looked at the board excitedly. She was on the cusp of beating her father. He made his move, the only move that he had left, and she quickly made hers, realising what she had done.

She had beaten her father.

"Tilly, my girl," her father exclaimed, his eyes widening. "Do you think you can do that again?"

Tilly scrunched her nose, retracing her steps in her mind. "I think so."

He nodded approvingly. "Show me again, then."

So, she did. Tilly beat her father again that night and every night afterward, not because he wasn't trying but because the game suddenly seemed easier to her. Her father encouraged her to find new moves, moves that were far more subtle and soon his smile was a little brighter, his laughter not as forced as it had been. "I always knew you were a child prodigy," he praised her, after every game she won.

Even Aunt Ruth came to watch her play and Tilly felt her cheeks flush as her father admired the way she played. "See, Ruthie?" he exclaimed when Tilly beat him soundly. "She's a natural I tell you! A natural!"

"Perhaps," her aunt responded, a hesitancy to her tone. "It is just a game though, George."

Her father met her aunt's gaze. "But this game has tournaments. I've read about them myself, in the local paper. My girl is better than most, I tell you."

Tilly watched as Aunt Ruth's expression fell and something akin to horror crossed her face. "No,

George, you aren't going to do that to your own daughter!"

"Do what?" Tilly interjected.

Her father looked at her and she was warmed by his broad happy smile. Her father would never hurt her. She trusted him. "Would you like to play someone else, Tilly, my girl?" he asked, his eyes twinkling mischievously.

"Who?" she asked tentatively. Her aunt had never bothered to sit in on their games until recently and no one else in the household, well those that were left, had seen a chess board before. Only Tilly and her father could play.

Her father's smile only grew, and Tilly found herself returning his grin. "Oh, Tilly, my girl," he finally said, clapping his hands together. "This is going to be the start of something good. Just you wait and see!"

Tilly glanced over to where her aunt sat, her lips firmly pressed in a line, and she sincerely hoped that it would be.

CHAPTER 2

The following week, Tilly was ambling idly down the hallway toward her father's study, when she heard her aunt's raised voice coming from beyond the half-closed door. Slowing her steps, Tilly pressed her small body against the dark panelled wall and listened intently.

"You cannot surely wish to do this!" her aunt was saying in hushed tones, her voice sharper than Tilly had ever heard before. "We don't have the funds for a gathering."

Her father scoffed. Tilly could almost imagine him waving a hand at her aunt, as if her concerns were trivial at best. "Funds? Funds can be procured, Ruthie."

"Procured?" her aunt challenged. "By whom? There is nothing else to sell in the house and we are barely able to put food on the table as it is! This should be reconsidered, George."

"I want some laughter in this household," her father demanded. "Something that will take our minds off our lack of funds and food. Ruth and a gathering is just the ticket, you will see."

Tilly heard her aunt sigh loudly. "George, please. You should be out there, looking for work, not organising a party."

"No one will have me," he said darkly. "You know that. I'm nothing more than a washed-up sea captain without a vessel. The young buck has put the word out about how incapable I am."

Tilly didn't think that her father was anything but a magnificent captain, able to steer the ships he commanded through the storms and mythical creatures he conjured up in her nightly bedtime stories. Shame on those who couldn't see what he was capable of!

"And what is the gathering going to bring to this house other than a bunch of drunken fools and deeper into debt?" her aunt asked. "It won't bring Gracie back."

"True, Gracie isn't here," he interrupted her, "but may I remind you that this is my house, remember, Ruth."

"Fine," she answered a moment later. "But don't be surprised at all when this is the ruin of you."

Tilly hurried away from the door and into the shadows of the hallway, watching as her aunt swiftly exited the study, her jaw clenched tightly. Once she was certain her aunt wasn't coming back, Tilly crept into the study, finding her father staring out the window, off into the distance. "Papa?" she asked cautiously.

He shook himself out of whatever deep thought he was in and gave her a gentle smile, motioning for her to come to him. Tilly did as he asked, and he pulled her up onto his knee. "Tilly, my girl, we are going to have a party," he announced, his large hand pressing onto her back. "And most of all, I want you to attend it and show everyone your abilities."

Tilly's breath caught. "Truly?" She had never attended a party before, and certainly not one that her father had hosted. Most of the time, she had been forced to her room, with her aunt muttering at her.

"Aye," he replied.

"May I have a new dress, Papa?" she asked hesitantly. When she and Aunt Ruth had gone to market the day before, Tilly had seen a pretty pale blue lacy outfit in one of the shop windows, it had a matching wide blue bow tied at the waist. It was perhaps the loveliest item she had ever seen.

"No," her father stated briskly. "But I do have another plan for you, Tilly, one that I know you will enjoy. Do you trust your dear old Papa?"

Tilly looked up at her father. "Of course, I do."

"Then you are going to enjoy this party," he exclaimed as he set her on her feet. "Now, run along. There is much preparation to be done!"

Tilly walked out of the study, her steps light. She was going to attend a party, a real party, with her Papa!

THE NIGHT of the party swiftly came along, and Tilly waited anxiously for her father to come to her room, clad in nothing more than her thin shift. She had prayed every night before bed that he would change his mind about a new dress and surprise her with the one she had seen, or something that he had picked up on his travels, to make her the envy of all the party guests. The household had been in a frenzy all week long, the meagre staff scrubbing, cleaning, and polishing every inch of the house until she could see her face in the surfaces. Her aunt had done nothing but fret and worry at the sheer amount of food and drink that had come through the doors, along with the additional staff that her father had hired, muttering that they were going to be in the poorhouse before the week ended.

Tilly didn't worry so much. Her father would never allow that to happen. She trusted him to keep them safe, secure, and happy, and this party was just one of the ways he was doing so.

Finally, when Tilly thought she couldn't wait a moment longer, the door opened and her father stood there, dressed in his grand evening finery. "Tilly, my girl," he stated, stepping in, a bundle tucked under his arm. "Are you excited about tonight?"

"Yes, Papa," Tilly answered, unable to hide her broadening smile. "Do you have something for me?"

"Aye, I do," he replied, handing over the bundle. "You are going to be an actress tonight, Tilly. Do you know what that means?"

Tilly took the package and inside found a pair of trousers and a waistcoat, along with a brown corduroy cap. "What is the meaning of this?" her aunt asked harshly peering from behind her father. "What are you doing, George?"

Her father ignored her aunt as he crouched before Tilly. "I want to play a trick on my friends, Tilly," he said softly, his eyes twinkling. "Do you want to help me with that trick?"

Hiding her hurt about not seeing any dress, Tilly gave him a hesitant smile. "I will help with whatever you need me to do, Papa."

"Good, Tilly, my girl," he reassured. "Put the clothes on. Ruth, make sure to bind her hair tightly under the cap. Tonight she is going to be Matthew."

"George," her aunt warned. "Matilda is a lovely girl. Why would you want her to be a boy?"

Why indeed? Tilly thought as her father straightened up. The clothes in her hands were coarse, lacking the frills and lace that she would have liked to wear for the party.

"I have a plan, Ruth," her father said, giving an encouraging smile to Tilly. "And Tilly is going to excel at it, I just know she is. She is clever and smart, something she got from Gracie."

The mention of her mother caused Tilly to lift her chin. Her father needed her help. Her help, not her aunt's or anyone else's. "I don't mind being Matthew for the party, Papa. If it will help you."

"Good!" her father exclaimed, clapping his hands together. "Then get dressed, my dear girl, and come to the great room when you are ready. Remember, you will be Matthew for the night."

After her father strode out of her room her Aunt Ruth tutted audibly. "There is nothing good that is going to come of this!"

Tilly wasn't listening, instead donning the clothes that her father had given her. She was small for her age, so the clothing was a little too large on her bird-like frame, but they would be simply fine for one evening. Aunt Ruth came over and started to bind

Tilly's hair into a tight bun on the top of her head. "Careful, Matilda," she said softly, jabbing the pins to hold her hair in place. "Anything that your father comes up with never pans out."

"It is just one night," Tilly said softly, letting her aunt place the hat securely on her head. With her hair hidden, she did have the appearance of being a boy, though there was nothing she could do to hide the shining excitement in her eyes. Her father needed her, and she wasn't going to let him down. Tonight, she would be the best actress in all of London!

Once she was dressed, her aunt walked her down the stairs where laughter, music and frivolities were already filling the air. Though their house was small, there were people at every turn, all eyeing her with curiosity as she passed by.

"There he is!" her father boomed, coming over to grasp Tilly's hand. "May I present my son, Matthew?"

"I didn't know you had a son," someone called out.

"Of course, I do," the captain said and grinned, pushing Tilly forward. "He's a sickly thing, like his mother was before him, so I have kept him safe from the frigid misty air for most of his life."

Tilly did her best not to frown. Her aunt had told her never to lie, but her father was lying with every word that came out of his mouth. No, not lying. This was a trick, and she was expected to play along, for his sake.

"At three," her father continued, gazing around the room, "he had already learned all his letters and was able to read, then at five, he was working on his algebra and now, at the age of eight, he has mastered the art of chess."

There was laughter and guffaws about the room. "Eight, you say?" one asked. "It is preposterous."

"I think you have had too much to drink, Captain," another replied before tipping up his own glass of brandy.

"I'm telling you the truth," he shot back, his brow furrowed. "And anyone who wants to prove me otherwise, I will wager against."

Tilly watched as several well-dressed gentlemen stepped forward, pulling money from their pockets. "One at a time," her father called out, leading Tilly to the chess board already set up in the middle of the room. "Don't be too eager for me to take your money."

"I would like to see you try," a man with a thick black moustache replied, his eyes set on Tilly. "What do you say, lad? Do you want to beat me at chess?"

Tilly looked up at her father who gave her an encouraging nod. She would do it for him.

SEVERAL HOURS LATER, Tilly scrunched her nose up as she traced the pattern with her eyes, looking for the best route to win. She had lost count of the games she had played, how many men she had beaten, but this one was proving to be the most difficult of them all. Lord Farthing was the man's name, a well to do gentleman who owned the shipping offices that her father had sailed out of. Unlike the rest, he had barely touched his glass that sat next to the chess board, concentrating hard, just as she had done for the other games. Tilly had found herself beginning to lose her first game of the evening.

"Well, well, Matthew?" Lord Farthing said smugly, drumming his fingers along the tabletop. "What is your next move going to be?"

Tilly made a rash decision, picking up her knight, one of the few remaining pieces she had left and moved it to its new position, watching intently as Lord Farthing's moustache rose in a smile. "Good choice," he replied, moving his piece to block her intent, taking away her knight. "But not the best, I'm afraid."

The room made a collective gasp and Tilly looked at the board, realising that she had been defeated. "Good game," the gentleman stated, pushing up from the chair. "You certainly have talent, Matthew, there is no doubt about that. Call upon me when you are ready to defeat me."

Tilly watched as the man weaved his way through the crowd, a dull roar pushing through her ears. She had lost.

She didn't like to lose.

Bills were exchanged before her father helped her out of the chair, a small frown on his face. "Go on up to your bedroom, Matthew."

She wanted to apologise to her father for disappointing him but the moment she opened her mouth their ruse would be up, and that would only further upset him.

So, she did as he asked, walking up the stairs to her room. There, her aunt was waiting and together they removed her clothing and the pins holding her hair tightly in place, letting it trail down her back. "Your fool of a father is going to get us all killed," Aunt Ruth muttered, sliding the night gown over Tilly's head. "Look at him, betting on his own flesh and blood! It surely is the devil's work!"

Tilly was too tired to respond, but she didn't fall asleep as soon as her head laid down on the pillow. Her mind was too alert and anxious, trying to find the mistake she had made when playing Lord Farthing and how she would beat him the next time they met.

The next morning, she went down to breakfast and found her father waiting for her. "You did good, Tilly, my girl."

"Thank you, Papa," she answered, glad that he was pleased with her. "I'm sorry I couldn't beat Lord Farthing."

"Pfft, you will in time," her father responded, clasping his hands behind his back. "Did you like playing, Tilly?"

Tilly thought about it for a moment. She enjoyed seeing their crestfallen expressions when they realised they had been beaten by her, at such a young age, too. Then there was the way her father had been delighted at Matthew's success. "Yes, Papa," she finally answered. "I did."

Her father smiled. "Good! Then I'm going to get you a tutor, Tilly, my girl, so that you can learn a few new moves. Would you like that?"

The chance to beat Lord Farthing one day... Yes, she would. "Yes, Papa."

"That's my girl," he said. "You helped your Papa last night, and your Aunt. The funds you won will pay off some of our debts."

Tilly preened under her father's praise. She was helping. She was making all of them happy by just playing chess.

"You can't possibly mean to continue this farce."

They both looked at Aunt Ruth who stood in the doorway, her lips pressed tightly together. "This is so very wrong, George. You, of all people, should know that."

Her father's smile faded. "I didn't see you complaining when I gave you the money this morning, Ruth. Where do you think that money came from?" He clasped a hand on Tilly's shoulder. "We have something here, Ruth, something that is going to secure our futures."

"I still don't like it," her aunt responded, her anger only growing. "If someone finds out what you are about, you will be ruined."

"Then, they don't find out," her father finished. "Tilly, you don't mind being Matthew again, do you?"

"No, Papa," she announced, lifting her chin defiantly. "I don't mind."

Her aunt made a sound of disgust before leaving the room, leaving them alone. "She will come around, don't you worry," her father murmured as he led Tilly over to the breakfast table. "You won't tell a soul, will you?"

Tilly climbed into the chair, her mouth watering at the food on the table. This morning there was steaming hot chocolate with freshly baked bread rolls, and bacon, the scent tickling her nose and she couldn't remember the last time she had tasted the sweet treat. "No, Papa. I promise."

"Well, then, it's decided," her father announced, picking up his fork and stabbing a crispy piece of bacon. "I will procure the tutor and you will learn how to beat Lord Farthing."

Tilly reached for her cup, carefully pouring the hot chocolate into it. She would learn how to beat Lord Farthing simply to keep her father happy.

CHAPTER 3

A FEW MONTHS LATER...

*T*illy wrinkled her nose as she studied her moves, carefully analysing each one as her tutor had taught her to. They were seated in Lord Farthing's study; the only sound was the ticking clock on the mantle and occasional pop from the burning wood in the fireplace. Her forgotten cup of hot chocolate sat at her elbow, along with Lord Farthing's glass of amber liquid, and after what had seemed like hours of play, she was nearing the end of the game.

It was a particularly important game at that. After months of daily tutoring from Mr Aaronovitch, an eminent math's professor, Tilly had begun to defeat him during their sessions. He had been delighted that she had taken his tutelage to heart and once her progress was shown to her father, he had promptly lined up a game with a certain gentleman she had yet to beat.

That game was today. Tilly had been nervous walking into the Lord Farthing's opulent household in London's Mayfair, marvelling at his sumptuous furnishings and lavish decorations. From the coach that had come to retrieve her and her father to the velvet cushion she was now seated upon, Tilly wished that she could give all that the man had to her father and her aunt.

"Careful now," Lord Farthing stated as Tilly's hand hovered over one of the pieces. "One move, Matthew, and the game will be over."

It was what she was betting on. Tilly quickly made her move and grinned triumphantly as she realised she had won the game. "You defeated me," he breathed, his eyes scanning the board. "You actually succeeded."

"I told you," her father's voice boomed from close by. "I told you that he would get to be good enough to beat you."

Tilly's smile broadened at her father's praise. She had studied hard and now she had finally done what she had waited months to do.

She had beaten Lord Farthing.

"Well, now," the gentleman finally said, leaning back in his chair. "I am impressed, Wainwright. You have a true protégé on your hands in your son."

Tilly's smile dimmed somewhat, looking at her father to see if he was going to correct the Lord. She wanted to be herself, no longer Matthew but just Tilly, a girl who had learnt how to play chess. The suits her father had put her in were no longer fun and with the funds that they had acquired, she wished for a new dress to wear.

"Aye," her father said proudly, his eyes set on Tilly. "My son truly is exceptional."

"I would like to hold a social event myself," Lord Farthing announced as he pushed out of his seat. "To showcase your son's talents. There are many people in London who would be intrigued to play against your son."

"Of course," her father replied. "We would like that."

"And you will be compensated for Matthew's attendance, of course," Lord Farthing continued as Tilly stared raptly at the two men, wanting to speak up but too afraid to do so.

The captain inclined his head. "That is very generous of you, My Lord."

So, it began. Tilly and her father returned to the opulent townhouse in London a fortnight later, finding it overrun with well-dressed gentlemen and women. Tilly followed her father through the throng of people, taking in the beautiful gowns of the women in attendance, her little heart wrenching in her chest. Here she was, clad in itchy woollen trousers and a coat to match, yet she longed to wear one of the colourful silk and satin dresses around her

It wasn't fair. Surely, they would be just as accepting of a girl with the talent she had as they had been when she was masquerading as a boy!

Although she said nothing as they were led into Lord Farthing's dining room, the table stretching nearly the length of room. "Welcome!" Lord Farthing called out, pressing a glass into her father's hand. "Is Matthew ready to play tonight?"

"As he always is," her father responded, placing his hand on Tilly's back. "Do you have suitable opponents?"

"Of course," the Lord said smoothly, gesturing towards the table. Tilly took in the sheer number of challengers waiting for her and swallowed. Were any of them as good as Lord Farthing?

Suddenly she didn't want to do this. The smell of her father's drink fuelled breath was making her feel ill, her palms began to sweat with the terror of everyone looking at her. This gathering was much larger than her father's party had been and if she didn't beat them all, he would be upset, and she would have let him down.

"Matthew?"

Tilly looked up at her father, seeing his frown. They had come a long way to have this night and if she told him she wished to leave, he would be even more upset with her.

"Perhaps a cup of hot chocolate for the lad?" Lord Farthing was asking, snapping his fingers at the maid.

Her father continued to stare at her, questions flickering in the depths of his eyes and Tilly drew in a deep breath. She couldn't ask him if they could leave. This gathering was for them.

So, she nodded, and he loosened a breath. "Stage fright!" He chuckled, pushing Tilly toward the table. "Get the hot chocolate! My son is ready to play!"

The crowd in the dining room grew larger after she defeated opponent after opponent, while enjoying the rich and creamy hot chocolate from a fragile teacup. The crowd cheered at her every time she finished a winning move and her adversaries started to grow apprehensive about even starting a game with her.

There was one time during the night, that her father lined up three opponents at once, all formidable adversaries who had likely been playing chess all their lives. "Watch as my son defeats them all!" he called out, pride in his voice. Tilly's cheeks flushed at the praise, knowing that she was making her father happy with each game she won.

It was nearly dawn by the time the crowd dispersed, and her father's cheeks were flushed with excitement and the alcohol he had imbibed as they climbed into their coach for their journey home. Tilly could barely keep her head up, exhausted from the long evening, but when her father threw his arm around her shoulder, she managed a sleepy smile. "You did good, Tilly, my girl," he boomed, hugging her to his side. "You made your dear Papa immensely proud tonight. Those gentle folks, well, they don't know what hit them, or their pockets."

"Am I helping you, Papa?" she asked drowsily, the lull of the coach causing her eyelids to droop.

"Aye, my girl, you are," he replied gently. "You most certainly are."

WITH LORD FARTHING'S ASSISTANCE, Tilly and her father found themselves in far more opulent drawing rooms around London over the next few weeks and months. Sometimes, Tilly played one or two opponents, sometimes more, but she beat them all with ease, causing her father's pockets to be flush with funds. Her aunt had protested more than once that her father should stop the charade while he could, but the invitations kept coming and soon the scratchy woollen suit she had been wearing was replaced with softer and finer material that made Tilly forget all about the lacy dresses in the shop window.

That and the gifts her father bestowed upon her encouraged her to continue. Dolls, beautiful chess boards, a mechanical boat from Lord Farthing, they all filled her room. Even the household started to improve, with more staff around and less that Aunt Ruth had to do herself. Their dinner table was laden with food each evening and Tilly's ever-present hot chocolate became a bedtime ritual whenever she wasn't out in the drawing rooms of London's elite.

One morning, when they were still enjoying breakfast, the butler brought a letter in, along with the other numerous invitations to social events. "Well, now," her father stated as he retrieved the missive, passing off the invitations to her aunt. "I wonder if our dear Matthew has garnered some more followers."

"When can I be Tilly again?" she asked lightly, pushing the coddled eggs around on her plate. "I want to wear dresses like the ladies do at the parties."

Her father glowered at her. "Now, Tilly, don't be stupid, what would happen if I took you along, a mere girl, instead of Matthew. The young lad that they are excited to see, would be no more?"

Her shoulders slumped. "Yes, they would be disappointed."

"And it would take some time to remind them what you can do," he prompted her as he tore open the envelope. "It is best that you remain as Matthew for now, Tilly, my girl."

"George, why don't you give the girl some time alone?" her aunt suggested, brushing aside the stack of invitations. "She's had quite a few late nights for weeks on end now and I'm worried about her lack of sleep. I know she is very capable at her lessons, but you really need to step back."

Her father wasn't listening to either one of them though. In fact, he had grown quite pale as his eyes scanned the contents of the letter before him. "What's wrong, Papa?" Tilly asked hesitantly, afraid that it was bad news.

He cleared his throat, hastily tucking the letter into his waistcoat pocket. "Nothing, my dear. Just some scoundrel telling me that he knows who and what you are."

Aunt Ruth gasped, her hand flying to her throat. "But George that is serious! He could send the law after you for duping all those people!"

"I didn't deceive anyone," her father replied tightly. "Tilly can play, and play well at that. The fact that she is a girl masquerading as a lad is nothing."

Her aunt frowned. "Then why not just let people know and be done with it? You just said it had nothing to do with her abilities."

Tilly's father ignored his sister-in-law, turning his attention on Tilly instead. "Tonight, Lord Farthing has a surprise for you, Tilly, my girl. You best go upstairs and rest up for the evening. I need you at your sharpest."

"Yes, Papa," she replied sliding out of her chair. It wasn't until she was back in her room, lying upon her bed, that Tilly allowed herself to think about her aunt's words. She was right, it shouldn't matter whether she was a girl or a boy. Her skills were the same either way.

Did Lord Farthing know she was a girl? Tilly didn't know that answer. If so, then surely, he would help her papa explain their ruse.

That evening, Tilly and her father found themselves in a large country estate on the outskirts of London. Tilly caught a glimpse of a large ballroom as they passed, couples swirling around to the music, in brightly coloured silks and satins on the dance floor. She sighed a little at the sight. She wanted to watch them all night, but her father urged her along the crowded corridor and Tilly was forced to think about what was expected of her. "There he is," Lord Farthing announced as they approached a tall gentleman dressed in evening coat tails. "Mr Pelletier, may I present Captain Wainwright and his very able son, Matthew."

The gentleman turned from his conversation, peering at Matthew through his gold rimmed spectacles. "So, this is the protégé I've heard so much about."

"Aye, this is my son," her father stated, pushing Tilly forward. "One of the best chess players in all of London."

"He beat me soundly," Lord Farthing added with a jovial laugh. "So, I would have to agree to that statement."

The two men laughed but Mr Pelletier continued to eye Tilly with an intense gaze. "Mr Pelletier is arguably the best chess player in the whole of France," Lord Farthing explained after their laughter subsided.

Tilly's father arched a brow. "Really?"

The Frenchman straightened his shoulders, making him impossibly tall. "Mais oui, but of course."

"Well, then," her father said after a moment, a broad smile on his face. "Why don't we organise an event and showcase some of the best chess players in all of London and France? You can go up against my son here and we can see who truly is the best player."

Tilly wanted to hide behind her father as the Frenchman's gaze hardened, clearly not at all impressed about taking on a mere child.

"It will make for good betting," Lord Farthing added, a pleased smile on his face. "It would be quite the show."

Mr Pelletier didn't look at all pleased with that prospect and Tilly swallowed. She didn't want to play this man. She wanted to go back to her dresses and tea parties with her aunt, to play with the toys she now had in her room and only play chess against her father whenever she chose to.

"A fine idea," her father finally said. "But first, we have business tonight."

Tilly was glad when they left the man behind, turning their attention to the evening's opponents instead. Perhaps her father would change his mind about this whole farce of an event, and she could go back to her life before she had ever moved a chess piece.

When they finally entered the coach to take them home, although she was exhausted, Tilly wasn't tired enough to not address the situation with her father. "I don't want to play that man."

Her father chuckled. "But why not, Tilly, my girl? Think of what it will bring to you and your family if you defeat him."

"You mean if Matthew defeats him," she corrected, snatching the hat off her head and throwing it on the floor of the coach. "I want to play like this Papa, as Tilly."

Her father tickled her under the chin. "You can't, Tilly, and that's the end of it, you hear? Do you not like your hot chocolates, and the finery that the money has brought? How do you think we are affording such luxuries?" he forced out.

She saw the anger in his eyes, and swallowing she pushed herself further back into the seat. "I'm sorry, Papa."

The anger faded and he pulled her close. "I'm not going to let anything happen to you. You are doing good, Tilly, my girl, really good. We have to keep the charade up for a little while longer, until all our debts are paid in full."

CHAPTER 4

The weeks passed and Tilly practiced every day for the event where she would play an actual professional chess player, working on the harder moves that her tutor had shown her.

Her father grew more morose as the days passed as Lord Farthing hadn't set a date for the event, promising to do so as soon as he could. "I don't understand," her father stated one night at dinner, his brow furrowing. "He seemed open to the idea."

"I don't think that you should go through with it," Aunt Ruth responded plainly as Tilly pushed her carrots around her plate. "It is just asking for trouble, George. We have sufficient funds now, surely."

"But those funds will not last for long," her father interrupted as he picked up his glass. Recently, Tilly had noted the fine brandy bottle was always seated next to her father's plate at dinner, recognising it from the many events she had attended with him. He seemed to indulge in it frequently and he became quite bleary eyed when he had imbibed too much. "Besides, Tilly is a protégé and we need to let everyone know," he said, slurring his words.

"You mean Matthew is," her aunt corrected him, her lips pulled down in a disapproving frown.

Her father waved a hand at her. "It is no matter."

It did matter to Tilly, though. She wanted them to see her pretty dresses and how she was just as smart as any boy could be.

A letter came with the post for her the next afternoon and Tilly held it excitedly in her hands. She had never received a letter of her own, and it made her feel rather grown up, as if she was important.

Hurriedly, she broke the seal and pulled out a single sheet of paper, unfolding it. Her smile died as she read its contents. *I know who you are and what you are doing. Don't make me let all of London know about your little ruse, as well.*

Her breath caught in her throat. Someone knew that she wasn't a boy!

When her father came home later that day, Tilly followed him into his study, watching as he grabbed the half empty decanter from the table. "Look at this, Papa," she said, offering him the letter. "Someone knows."

Her father snatched the letter out of her grasp, his skin growing pale. "This means nothing," he grumbled, throwing the letter into the fire. Tilly gasped as she watched the paper's edges curl from the heat. "But, Papa," she tried again.

Her father rounded on her, his eyes flashing. "Don't breathe a word about this, Tilly, not to anyone. It means nothing."

Tilly swallowed her retort, but instead of comforting her like he had in the past, he turned his back and poured himself a glassful of the comforting amber liquid, draining it in one solid movement.

Tears stung her eyes and Tilly backed out of his study, hurrying to her room instead. Her father had never reacted to her that way before. She knew he was worried about Lord Farthing's promise of the upcoming chess event, but after receiving that letter, perhaps it was time to listen to her aunt and cease their pretence.

Perhaps her father could say that Matthew had retired from playing chess and was concentrating on his schoolwork, and Tilly could emerge as the next player. Then they wouldn't be deceiving anyone. After all, she was just as smart as any boy could be and she had already proven herself to have the ability to defeat nearly any opponent that she came across.

It would be a way to have London society forget about her 'brother' and focus on her, without having to wear the boy's clothing she was forced to dress in.

Tilly decided to inform her father of her thoughts the very next evening, but Aunt Ruth wanted just the two of them to eat their meal together, instead of with her father. "Lord Farthing is here," she stated briskly. "Your father is busy, Matilda."

Matilda stuck out her lower lip and after dinner was finished, she decided that she would still see him, and Lord Farthing, to tell them of her thoughts.

Once her aunt tucked her in for the night, Tilly waited until she was certain that her aunt had retired to bed for the night before she snuck out of her room and down the stairs, careful to avoid the creaking parts of the stairs in the process.

As she drew close to his study, Tilly could hear the raised voices of her father and Lord Farthing spilling out into the hallway.

"I can't believe you lied to me!" Lord Farthing raged. "Do you not know who I have spoken to on your behalf? Do you realise what you have done to me?"

"It's one bloody letter!" her father growled. "A coward by the looks of it." Tilly pressed herself flat against the wall, her heart beating rapidly in her chest. Was her father talking about her letter or another that he had received?

"A coward that can ruin you and me both!" Lord Farthing shot back. "I will be the laughingstock all over town for this!"

"I can fix this," her father replied, a hint of panic in his voice. "Don't be concerned, I can fix this."

Tears stung Tilly's eyes as she listened to her father plead with the Lord, wishing that she had never agreed to be Matthew. If she hadn't, then her father wouldn't be in such a state now.

There was a crash of glass to the floor and Tilly jumped at the sound. "You can't fix this!" Lord Farthing roared. "I will have your head for this, Wainwright! You will not make me a mockery because of your insolence!"

"My insolence?" her father replied. "There is nothing that I haven't done to make you successful, Farthing! You willingly went along with this."

"What I went along with," Lord Farthing replied, "is supporting a chess player that was a boy, not a girl! They will never believe that you hid her for any good reason! They will think that they were hoodwinked and if you were expecting some sort of jest to be overlooked, then you are wrong, Wainwright! People don't take kindly to being made a fool of and you are about to find out how wrong you were in doing so!"

Tilly didn't want to hear anything else. She ran from the hall and back up the stairs, not bothering to dodge the creaky steps this time. Instead of running directly into her room, she headed for Aunt Ruth's room. Aunt Ruth was always the calm one, the rational one of the house, and she would know what to say.

Her aunt's door was slightly ajar as Tilly approached it and when she pushed it open, she found her aunt standing by the window, tears streaming down her cheeks. Tilly had never seen her aunt cry before, and the scene caused her to gasp aloud.

Aunt Ruth turned sharply, her eyes widening. "What are you doing out of bed, Matilda?"

"Papa is fighting with Lord Farthing," Tilly's words spilled out, not caring that her aunt was going to be upset with her for leaving her bedroom. "He needs help."

"Go to your room, Matilda," her aunt replied coldly, dashing at the tears on her cheeks and bringing about the stoic expression that Tilly knew well. "It is none of your concern."

Tilly bit her lower lip. It was her concern. Her father and Lord Farthing were fighting because of her, because of what they had done, and she wanted to tell them her thoughts. "But, Aunt."

"Go!" her aunt shouted, Tilly flinching at the sound. Her aunt had never raised her voice at Tilly like that before.

She turned and ran into her room, shutting the door behind her. Her chest heaved and the tears that began to roll down her cheeks were of both anger and fear. Something was wrong. Something had reduced her aunt to tears and caused her father to beg for Lord Farthing's forgiveness.

Tilly sat against the door for what seemed like hours, waiting for the moment that either her father or her aunt would come to check on her.

Neither came and after the clock in the hall chimed midnight, Tilly climbed into her bed, pulling the covers up around her chin. Tomorrow, she would tell her father what they could do to make this all right.

The next morning, Tilly awoke to find the sky grey and dull, the threat of rain looming. She threw back the covers and padded to the door, opening it to find the house deathly silent.

Tilly made her way down the stairs to the dining room and frowned as she didn't see their normal breakfast fare laid out on the table or her father seated in his usual chair, reading the morning paper.

"Matilda."

Tilly turned and found Aunt Ruth behind her, her face swollen, her eyes red. "What is it?" she asked immediately, coldness seeping into her body. Something was wrong. Something was amiss. "Where's Papa?"

Her aunt cleared her throat as she knelt in front of Tilly, placing her hands on her shoulders. "Matilda, something has happened."

"What is it?" Tilly asked, her hands fisting at her sides. "Does this have to do with Lord Farthing?" He had seemed terribly angry last evening.

"Matilda," her aunt tried again, a catch in her throat. "Your father... there was an accident last night and he, well, it would appear that he used his own pistol to shoot himself."

For a moment, the words didn't register with Tilly. Her father was the wonderful Captain Wainwright, nothing could stop him.

Absolutely nothing. Shot himself? Her father was excellent at handling his weapons. She had seen him do so many times before, carefully cleaning and reassembling them with such ease that Tilly found it hard to think he would have done so accidentally. "You're lying," she told her aunt, attempting to pull away from her grasp. "Papa!"

"I'm not lying to you," Aunt Ruth started to say as Tilly succeeded in wrenching herself away from her aunt. "No, Matilda. Don't!"

But Matilda was already heading to her father's study, knowing that she would find him seated behind his desk instead, poring over his ledgers.

There was a rumble behind her, but she didn't stop, pushing the door open and rushing into the room she knew so well.

It was empty. "Papa!" she cried out. "Papa!"

No answer. Tilly turned to go but it was then that something caught her eye, causing her to pause.

It was a large circular blood stain, on the rug that her father had kept in front of his desk. Her body trembled now, as she moved closer to the mark, finding more on the chair that she had often seen him sit in, the same chair that she herself had curled up in whenever she wished to spend time with him.

"Matilda," her aunt stated, pulling her away from the chair and placing her arm around Tilly's small shoulders. "Oh, my darling girl, you shouldn't be in here."

"He's not gone," Tilly whispered, her eyes still on the blood stain. "He can't be gone."

"He is," Aunt Ruth stated softly, guiding Tilly out of the study. There were others around, servants that had been loyal to the family, to the captain, even when he had no means to pay them, and all were looking at Tilly with the same, sorrowful expression.

Tilly let out a meek cry and pulled away from her aunt, racing for the stairs. This had to be a dream. If she could just make it back to her bedroom, then she would awake from this horrible nightmare and her father would be fine.

Sobbing now, Tilly pushed open the door to her room and flung herself onto the bed, pressing her face into her pillow. She needed to go to sleep. She had to go to sleep.

But sleep didn't come. Tilly allowed the tears to flow from her eyes and wet her pillowcase, all her hopes and dreams withering away with each passing moment.

Her father, her papa, was gone. She would never hear his laughter again, never see him smile at her proudly when she made the right chess move.

He wouldn't give her a nod of encouragement or come through the door so she could embrace him tightly, inhaling the scent of the sea that always seemed to cling to his clothing.

He was gone...

CHAPTER 5

illy stared down at the hole in the ground, the rain plopping on the dry earth, making the mud as dark as the dress she was wearing. Someone, a gentleman she didn't even know, held the umbrella over her head to keep the rain from soaking her thoroughly but Tilly didn't care so much.

Aunt Ruth cried softly into her handkerchief as the priest droned on about heaven and that her father was now with the Lord, but Tilly didn't believe that at all. She believed that her father's spirit was still in the household, ready to watch over them both.

Or at least that was what she hoped for. He had yet to come and comfort her, wipe her tears away, and tell her that everything was going to be all right. She needed for him to do that. Others had tried to comfort her, tried to tell her how much her father had loved and cared for her, but if he had, why did he take his own life and leave her behind in this world?

Their household had been an endless stream of mourners for days, coming to peer at her father's closed coffin and whisper about what he had done.

That wasn't the only whispers she had heard. Tilly hadn't bothered to put on her disguise and Aunt Ruth hadn't forced her to do so either, but she heard the rumours, the whispers about what her father had done to her and made her do.

They looked at her as if she was a ghost, instead.

She detested it all. Tilly despised the way that they had continued to ogle at her, how they smirked and shook their heads whenever the whispers grew. It mattered not that her father, her papa, was dead to them.

They wanted to watch their downfall. It hadn't taken long for Tilly to understand what her aunt had meant when she had stated that her father had shot himself. It wasn't an accident at all, he had meant to do so.

He had committed suicide. Tilly had heard the rumblings, how her father's soul would be doomed because he had taken his own life and she tried not to believe any of it.

Yet her father had done the deed. He had put the bullet in his own body that had taken him away from her and she didn't know if she would ever be able to forgive him for that. It was a selfish thought, but he had left her.

"Matilda," her aunt stated softly, bringing Tilly back to the present. "It is time."

Tilly drew in a deep breath and stepped back from the hole in the ground, watching as the men stepped in to lower the shiny oak coffin that held her father's body. Her aunt had dressed him in his captain's uniform, refusing to allow Tilly to help. "You don't want to see him like this," her aunt had chided softly, pushing her out of the room. "You want to remember him as he was."

Tilly didn't mind so much. She wanted to make certain that it was her father and not an imposter, pretending to be him. She wanted to believe that perhaps her father had taken off in the middle of the night on a ship after the row with Lord Farthing, faking his own death, and planning to return when the gossip died down.

Turning away from the men and their work, she followed her aunt back down the path that led out of the cemetery and to the waiting coach.

Lord Farthing's coach to be exact. While the Lord hadn't attended the small graveside service, Tilly thought it was good of him to send his coach for this dreary, wet day.

The household was quiet when they arrived back home, and Aunt Ruth removed her gloves with a sigh. "The meal is prepared, Matilda."

Tilly nodded and followed her into the dining room, where the food had been laid out on the table in anticipation for their return. She tried and failed to ignore the empty chair at the head of the table where her father would normally sit. "I don't want you to fret over what will happen next," her aunt started the moment that they sat. "I will figure this out. Once the gossip dies down, all will be well once more."

Tilly could only hope so.

～

THE WEEKS PASSED without much of a fuss. Tilly spent her days playing chess with invisible partners in her room, staying to herself and out of the way of her aunt. She wanted to find solace in her chess, but there wasn't a game that she didn't play that didn't bring tears to her eyes.

Tilly watched from the banister as her aunt let the staff that her father had hired go, tearfully explaining that they no longer had the funds to pay them. That and the creditors had started knocking on their door.

The first time it had happened, Tilly had thought it was more of her father's associates coming to check on how they were, but when she overheard her aunt's explanation that they didn't have any funds to give them, she realised that her father hadn't used any of the money that Tilly had won to pay off his debts, only adding to them. There were still debts from the original party he had thrown, and the fine brandy that he had drank far too often.

Tilly heard the creditors ask for all sorts of payment, one that had her cheeks redden in embarrassment as she realised the man was asking for her to join his household to work off her father's debts. The leering grin he had given her had made her want to wash in a tub full of icy water immediately.

Then items began to disappear from around the house. She watched as Aunt Ruth started to hand ornaments and furniture over to those who had come to reclaim their lost monies. The clock that had sat on the mantle in the sitting room or the fine pair of swords that had hung over the fireplace in the study disappeared. More and more Tilly started to notice that the household was becoming emptier and one morning in particular, she realised her best chess set, given to her by her father, was missing. "Where did my chess set go?" she asked her aunt at breakfast, which was nothing more than a bowl of porridge sweetened with the last of the cinnamon spice.

Aunt Ruth swallowed her mouthful. "I had to sell it, Matilda, to pay off one of your Papa's debts. I know you loved it, but it brought in a good price and kept the creditor's away for a little longer."

Tilly let the spoon slide back into the bowl. "That was given to me by Papa!"

Her aunt flinched at Tilly's sudden outburst and for a moment, Tilly saw the hurt in her aunt's eyes, making her feel bad about shouting. "Remember, your Papa is the reason I had to sell it," her aunt informed her after a tense moment. "I get no satisfaction in what I am doing, Matilda, but it is necessary in order for us to stay in this house a little while longer."

"I'm sorry, Aunt Ruth," Tilly mumbled, ashamed that she had spoken so strongly over a simple chess set.

"It is fine." Aunt Ruth sighed, reaching across to pat her hand. "This is hard for the both of us. I should have stepped in sooner and stopped your father." She drew in a breath, straightening. "It is too late now to be worried about it, though. We will do what we need to in order to survive, Matilda. I will not see us put out on the streets."

Tilly believed her aunt and time passed, but the creditors didn't stop coming. One particular afternoon, Tilly watched as her aunt left her father's study, showing a gentleman to the door. When she turned, she spied Tilly on the staircase. "I've got some sad news," she stated, clearing her throat. "We must sell the house."

Tilly's breath caught in her throat. "Where are we going to live?" Her aunt had promised her that they wouldn't be put out on the streets!

Aunt Ruth placed her hands on Tilly's shoulders, squeezing them gently. "We must sell the house. Your father placed a loan on the property some time ago without telling me and now the creditors are here for payment." Then she smiled and Tilly was surprised by it. She hadn't seen her smile since before her father had died. "But there is some good news, I have accepted a proposal of marriage; from a fine gentleman I knew long ago, before you were even born. He wants us to move into London with him."

London... Tilly gasped as she thought about the glittering city and all its finery that she had experienced on her jaunts with her father. Were they going to live in a palace just like Lord Farthing had? Perhaps this was going to work out after all!

Aunt Ruth knelt in front of Tilly, giving her a kind smile. "You are my responsibility now, Matilda, and I don't plan on shying away from that duty. Your mother, well, she would have wanted me to ensure that you were taken care of and since you are all that I have left of her, I plan on giving you the best life I can."

Tilly felt her eyes burn with tears and she threw her arms around her aunt's neck, glad that she hadn't been left alone by her father's death. "Oh, thank you, Aunt Ruth."

Her aunt returned her embrace, patting Tilly gently on her back. "Of course, my dear girl. We will get through this. You will see."

Pulling back, Tilly saw that her aunt was smiling. "Tobias is coming over for dinner tonight," she said, a hint of excitement in her eyes. "I would like to introduce you to him."

"I would like that very much," Tilly answered, glad to see her aunt happy at last. Tilly knew she wasn't the only one who had lost her father and now that they were on the verge of being destitute, her aunt was trying to be resourceful for their future.

Tilly could also be inventive. She would help her aunt wherever she could and if it meant saying goodbye to her childhood home, then she would do it.

That evening, Tilly watched as her aunt greeted a tall, slender gentleman at the door, blushing as he brushed his lips over her cheek. He was handsome enough, with a thatch of wayward blonde hair that seemed to forever fall in his eyes.

"Oh, this is Matilda," her aunt replied, stepping back so Tilly could move forward.

She had worn her best dress and she toyed with the fraying ribbon, meeting the gentleman's startlingly blue eyes with her own. "Matilda," he said, giving her a hesitant smile. "I'm Tobias Higson."

"You may call me Tilly," Tilly replied courteously.

His smile deepened. "Then you should call me Toby."

She liked him already.

They made their way into the dining room and her aunt served the meagre meal they had scraped together, blushing every time Toby's hands brushed across hers. Tilly had never seen her aunt like this before and it warmed her heart. Her aunt deserved to be just as happy as anyone else. "Are we really going to live in London?" Tilly asked with hope in her voice.

The two adults exchanged looks before her aunt gave Tilly a slight smile. "Of course, we are, but you should know that Toby is a simple gardener, Matilda."

Tilly's smile dimmed. A gardener. That was quite different from having a home such as Lord Farthing had, that would allow for Tilly to play chess.

"Our house is going to be sold next week," her aunt said, oblivious to Tilly's thoughts.

"Then we should wed by the end of the week," Toby replied, spearing his paltry piece of meat with his fork. "Then I can move you both to London immediately."

"Won't that be exciting!" her aunt exclaimed.

"Yes," Tilly said dully, pushing her food around her plate. "It will." She had hoped it would be the London she remembered, the wonderful ballrooms, glittering chandeliers and the colourful ballgowns she had seen once upon a time, but a gardener couldn't possibly have a large enough house to have a ballroom in it, could he?

The adults kept discussing their plans and Tilly tried not to dwell on what she had learnt. Her aunt had told her long ago that she should be thankful that she had a roof over her head and food in her belly. At least her aunt wasn't leaving her behind, and since Tilly had no one else to turn to then she would have to prepare herself for her new life, even if it wasn't quite what she wanted.

CHAPTER 6

*T*rue to her aunt's word and that of Toby's, they were wed by the end of the week in the local chapel, the verger and the vicar's wife acting as witnesses. Tilly stood proudly at her aunt's side as she said her vows, clutching the small bouquet of flowers she had picked from the little garden at the back of the house.

Tilly couldn't help but think how happy her aunt looked nor how the couple stole glances at each other as the vicar pronounced them wed.

After a chaste kiss, they returned home for a small wedding breakfast, Tilly the only one in attendance. How she wished that her aunt could have had a lavish wedding! After everything she had done for

Tilly, trying to make ends meet the best she knew how, she deserved a wonderful future.

As Tilly watched the couple interact with each other, she realised that her aunt was genuinely happy with Tobias. "Well," Aunt Ruth stated after they had finished their meal. "I guess we should start loading our few belongings onto the wagon."

"We do have a rather long journey to London." Toby grimaced as he pushed away from the table. "And I would like to be there by nightfall."

"Tilly," her aunt said as she stood. "Go change into an old dress and then we will start bringing our bags down the stairs."

"Yes, Aunt Ruth," Tilly responded, taking the stairs up to her room. Most of her belongings had either been given to the creditors or sold off to put food on the table, but her aunt had allowed her to keep a few items that she knew her father had given her. A plain chess set had been packed away in its case and waited by the door. It wasn't the best one but at least she could still play the game. The doll that her father had bought for her waited on her bed. She wore a pretty pink gown and had a jaunty bow in her brown woollen hair.

Tilly's trunk had already been packed by her aunt and the gown that Tilly was to put on after the wedding was hanging in the empty wardrobe. Drawing in a breath, Tilly crossed the room and quickly changed into the ordinary dress, folding the lace covered dress carefully in her hands and placing it in the trunk. Her heart was heavy at leaving the house today, the one place that held the memories of her father, but they had no other choice. He had caused them to have to leave the household. She realised that now.

Methodically, Tilly started moving the rest of her belongings near to the front door, keeping the tears at bay. Tears weren't going to help her now.

Still, as she passed by her father's study, Tilly couldn't help but take one last peek at the room that her father loved more than anything. The room itself was emptied, having been shut off as they had no further use for it.

Her father's scent of tobacco and the sea still hung in the air and Tilly took a moment to breathe it in. Once they left the house, it would be harder for her to remember what her father had smelt of and the comforting sounds and hugs he would give her whenever she was upset.

In time, she wouldn't even remember his face.

Tears crowded her eyes again and Tilly forced them back, stepping out of the room and shutting the door firmly behind her. This part of her life was over and now she had to look forward to the future, to a less than ideal life with her aunt and new uncle.

Perhaps it wouldn't be so bad, she thought as she made her way to the front door. After all, she would be living in London, amongst those who had watched her play with such rapt attention.

IT TOOK a few weeks for Tilly to grow used to her new life in London. Toby's home was actually a small set of rooms near London's East End, though the property was more respectable than most. Thankfully, Tilly found herself with her own room with one small window that she could almost see the city from.

It seemed that the city was always busy with the hustle and bustle of people moving to and fro along the pavements at all times of day and night. Whereas the small seaside village on the outskirts of London that they had lived in with her father had been quiet most of the time, the city was most definitely not. There was the ever-present sound of horses in the streets, or people nearby who's voices invaded Tilly's room.

Her room was sorely lacking the comforts that she had been used to before her father's death. There was no plush carpet for her to bury her feet in to ward off the chill of the morning or the cozy fireplace that would warm the room before she stepped foot out of bed.

Instead, she had a tightly woven rag rug to at least keep her bare feet from touching the cold wooden floorboards and a coal brazier that never seemed to stay lit long enough to warm the room.

As miserable as she was, Tilly tried not to complain. It was clear that her aunt was in love with her new husband, and she was trying to ensure that Tilly didn't end up working in some grimy factory, or worse. Tilly knew she should be grateful for the sacrifices that her aunt had made on her behalf. She could have easily married Toby and left Tilly behind or placed her in the workhouse.

Furthermore, Toby was obviously infatuated with her aunt. He was a hard worker, one that worked from sunup to sundown to provide for his new family. While he never seemed to have much to say, Tilly preferred his quiet nature most days.

As the days turned into months, Tilly learned more about the area they lived in and what Toby did to provide for their family. It had started out with a visit with her aunt to his place of work, Battersea Park, in the midst of London and not far from the opulent homes of London town.

The first time they had visited the park, Tilly had breathed in the fresh air and smiled at the sunlight on her face, giddy with excitement from seeing the London she had remembered with her father.

Sure enough, she could see the large, sumptuous houses in the distance as they entered the park, that contained well-dressed men and women milling about enjoying the warmth of the day. Though she was dressed in one of her best dresses for the outing, Tilly still felt as if she were wearing rags as she watched the other children with their governesses strolling along the pathways.

Toby had been excited to take them to the park, using his lunch break to show them around while he ate the sandwich that her aunt had brought for him.

It was clear to Tilly that Toby enjoyed his work and the twinge in her chest increased as she thought about how much she had enjoyed playing chess as well. She hadn't opened her chess set since they had moved, choosing to push it under the bed frame so that she would forget about it for a while.

After all, chess wasn't going to bring her the same bout of happiness without her father's presence and her dressing up as Matthew. Tilly knew that her aunt frowned upon any notion of Tilly pretending to be anyone other than herself and she didn't want to upset her aunt.

Still, in her dreams, Tilly was herself and playing chess against some of the best in all of Europe, especially Mr Pelletier. She would beat them soundly each time and they would chant her name as the pound notes would pile up on the table, far more than Tilly had ever seen.

One morning, while they ate breakfast, Toby cleared his throat. "Tilly, would you like to come to work with me today?"

Tilly looked up, surprised. "Truly?"

Aunt Ruth placed a hand on her husband's arm, seemingly surprised as well. "Are you certain, Toby? Won't she be in the way?"

Tilly held her breath. She didn't want to spend another day cooped up with her aunt, learning her numbers, letters, and how to darn a sock. To be outside, breathing in the fresh air—it would be something different indeed!

"Aye she will be of some help," Toby replied, his eyes on Tilly. "That is, if she would like to join me."

"Yes!" Tilly exclaimed, excited at the prospect of something new and different.

That day, Tilly learned about the different plants and flowers around the park and what it took to keep them looking beautiful. While Tilly paid attention to what Toby was saying, she couldn't help think about the large homes that she coveted, wishing that she were on an afternoon stroll with her father rather than working alongside the only father figure she would know for the rest of her days.

More than once she saw the glances in her direction and instead of ignoring them, Tilly pretended to pick the flowers, as if she were more than just hired help.

Toby saw it as if she were concentrating on her work and when they came home after one particular day in the park, he shyly presented her with a set of books. "This is how I learnt the art of gardening," he informed her softly as he handed her the well-worn books. "They have served me well."

Tilly took the books, her hand running over the tattered leather cover. "Are you certain this is good for her?" her aunt asked.

"Aye, that it is," Toby announced, snaking his arm around his wife's shoulders. "It won't hurt for her to know more than just chess moves and her numbers, Ruth. She's taken a real interest in what I do."

Tilly didn't correct him as to why she liked to go to the park and one afternoon, when the rain was far too hard for either of them to be outdoors, Tilly opened one of the books. For hours she pored over the names of the flowers, studying the crude drawings, trying to commit them to memory. With her clever mind she was soon able to point out the flowers to Toby's delight and together they found a common interest in discussing them when Tilly accompanied him to the park.

The months turned into years and after three years of being in London, Aunt Ruth unexpectedly and excitedly found herself with child. "I... I don't know how this happened," she informed Tilly one day, her hand resting on her still flat stomach. "I've never, I mean, I'm not young anymore."

The glow on her aunt's face was hard not to notice and Tilly was happy that her aunt had found something out of the tragedy that had befallen her in years past. Together they watched her girth increase until the day came that her labour pains began, and the birthing woman was called to their home.

To all their surprise, Aunt Ruth gave birth to not one but two healthy sons, both with the same blonde hair of their father. They named them Hugh and Francis, after Toby's two, now deceased, uncles and Tilly was moved to a room on the second floor to allow for the nursery to be closer to her aunt's room. "I hope you don't mind," Toby murmured as he helped Tilly move her belongings to the small dingy attic room. "I wish we had more space."

"It is fine," she stated, biting her lower lip as she surveyed the tiny space. Though small, it gave her a better view of the city she had come to love and a might more privacy than before.

After the birth of the two boys, the household changed. Her aunt was now busier than ever in raising her babies and Tilly often had to stay behind to help out instead of going with Toby.

Not that she minded. The babies were quite loud, but Tilly did enjoy watching them grow and develop and as the months passed, they learned to babble instead of cry, their smiles brightening the room whenever she entered.

Tilly's favourite time was at night, when she would help rock the boys to sleep, humming the familiar tunes that her aunt had used to sing to her as a child. When her aunt didn't need her help, Tilly studied the books that were quickly becoming her favourites, learning all that there was to know about the plants and flowers that Toby cared for, and some he didn't. Tilly found it a little like chess, learning the small pieces that would help her remember how to recognise them and then using her skills in the times that she was able to visit the park. Toby praised her for her knowledge and Tilly flourished under his praise, feeling the same flutter in her stomach that she had felt when she played chess with her father.

Over time, she slowly forgot about her time as Matthew and the game of chess, occupying her mind with familiar flora. Tilly became exceptionally good at working out which flowers and plants complimented others, garnering some attention from the more experienced gardeners that worked at the park. They would even ask her opinion on where to plant a particular shrub so that it flattered its neighbours.

It was then that she met Mr Myers, a flower shop owner who resided and worked on the fringe of Battersea Park. He had a flower cart from which he sold his wares and he had spied Tilly working alongside Toby.

CHAPTER 7

TEN YEARS LATER...

"*B*ut I don't want to work in the gardens any longer!"

Tilly stormed through the small home, removing her coat as she did so, her aunt hot on her heels, having started the same conversation that she always did when Tilly returned home from work.

"Then what are you going to do?" Aunt Ruth demanded, her hands on her hips. "You don't wish to get married. You don't want to work in the gardens. I will not have my niece working in a filthy factory for the rest of her days!"

Tilly whirled around, facing her aunt. "I don't plan on working in a factory and I haven't found anyone worth marrying yet!"

Aunt Ruth sighed. "Matilda, please. You are old enough now. Most women..."

Tilly shook her head, knowing exactly what her aunt was about to say. "I am not like the others out there. I will not be satisfied with simply being someone's wife." She swallowed hard. "I've been speaking with Mr Myers. He is going to allow me to work in his flower shop." After years of learning all she could about horticulture, as well as perfecting her floral arrangements, she was on the verge of finally doing something with her life.

"Mr Myers?" her aunt asked, surprised. "Whatever are you talking about?"

Tilly drew to her full height, lifting her chin. "Mr Myers has asked me to become his apprentice and I've accepted. I'm moving into his property by the end of the week." She had wanted to tell her aunt in a different manner, but given their heated discussion, it seemed as if now was as good a time as any. "I truly appreciate all you have done for me," she continued, her voice growing softer. "And what you and Toby have provided for me, but now it is time for me to leave."

Aunt Ruth's face dropped. She looked flabbergasted by Tilly's words, opening and closing her mouth several times without a word coming out. "I... I don't know what to say," she finally said.

"There is nothing to say," Tilly replied evenly. She had been quite excited to hear that Mr Myers thought her skills were good enough to work in his small shop, situated on the corner of a busy thoroughfare. When she had visited his shop, she had seen the well-dressed patrons of her past, the ladies with their lovely dresses and lacy parasols to block out the sun. The gentlemen wore top hats and had pocket watch chains swinging on their waistcoats. It all reminded her so much of her time with her father that Tilly's heart ached.

Most importantly, they frequented the shop regularly. When she had approached Mr Myers about helping in the shop, he had informed her that growing flowers was what she was best at. Recently he was beginning to realise her worth, especially as he was becoming a little older.

She had cajoled him enough to put her most recent flower arrangement in his shop window for one week to see if it would sell. If it didn't, she would leave him alone.

He had agreed and to both their surprise, it had been purchased within a matter of hours. Mr Myers had grumbled that it was beginner's luck, so she had provided him with another, and it had sold just as quickly.

Tilly had done all she could not to grin like a fool when he had begrudgingly asked her to continue to provide the arrangements and begin work behind the counter. Mr Myers had given her another task for the following week, and she had spent her time smiling to the well to do customers as she explained the differences between the flowers, such as the ones that would keep alive longer and set off the best fragrances. At the end of the week, he had been impressed enough to give into her demands and offer her what she had wanted for so long.

Freedom... Tilly was about to have her freedom. "He's given me a room over his shop," Tilly continued, clearing her throat. "I will be properly chaperoned by his daughter. He's going to pay me well, Aunt Ruth, it will be something to do with my hands and my mind."

Her aunt turned away and Tilly's shoulders slumped. She knew she had disappointed her by springing the news on her so suddenly. She couldn't very well take up a full-time gardening position with Toby. He had struggled hard enough to have her assist him, as this was not a job thought to be suited to women—dirty and full of hard labour.

Not that Tilly had minded much. She had always loved the feel of the earth sifting through her fingertips, watching as the plants and flowers she had devotedly placed in the soil flourished under her careful attention. Tilly also knew that Toby enjoyed the same and while he could never be her father, he had been a fine replacement for her over the years.

Now, though, it was time for her to forge her own path, make her own way, one that she could control.

Her aunt pursed her lips, crossing her arms over her chest. "I will be speaking about this to Toby."

Tilly notched her chin upward. "It doesn't matter. I'm not your daughter nor your ward anymore." Her words came out harsher than she had intended, and she saw her aunt flinch. Tilly wanted to apologise immediately as she saw the hurt on Aunt Ruth's face, but she kept her mouth closed. What she had said was the truth and no matter how much it hurt; her aunt knew it too.

Tilly turned on her heel and headed up to her attic room. For ten years she had watched London bustle past through the small window, wishing for the days that she had experienced with her father and now she could start anew with her position with Mr Myers. He could give her something that her aunt or Toby couldn't, exposure to those who had once looked at her in awe.

Even if they had thought she was a boy all along.

That evening, Tilly stayed in her room throughout dinner, sulking, as her father would have called it. She had not meant to hurt her aunt's feelings. In truth she appreciated everything that Aunt Ruth and Toby had done for her.

Her aunt didn't understand, though, how hard it had been for Tilly, especially to know that there wasn't anything she could have done to save her father. Now, even though he was gone, she still wanted to please him. He had been so happy with her when she was playing chess and winning.

She wanted to please him still. Not only that, Tilly wanted to feel that rush of pleasure knowing she had done something more, something to have her peers no longer look down upon her but as someone who perhaps could be their equal.

It was something her aunt couldn't understand.

It wasn't her aunt, though, that came to visit her that evening, a tray of dinner in his hands. Toby stared at her from the doorway, having changed from his dirt covered overalls that he favoured when working in the park to a pair of patched trousers and a clean shirt. "Can I come in?"

Tilly nodded and he stepped through the threshold, his head brushing the eaves. After setting down the tray on her bed, he stepped back. "Ruth told me what you are planning to do."

She sniffed. "And I imagine you are disappointed."

Toby took in a deep breath. "No, I'm not disappointed. Actually, I'm pleased for you."

Surprised, Tilly stared at her step-uncle. "You are?" She had thought that he would have the same hard feelings that her aunt had about the idea.

He quirked a small smile. "You have far surpassed any thoughts that I had of you from the moment you joined me in the park. You're a bright, quick learner,

Matilda, and I can't be more pleased of what you have achieved."

Tilly dropped her arms, tears springing to her eyes. Toby had never been one to give her much praise. He had always been a quiet, unassuming sort who had let her aunt do most of the talking.

But to hear that he was pleased with her, almost proud of her, meant more to Tilly than she could imagine. "I don't know what to say," she finally said, clearing her throat.

He waved a hand at her. "I just wanted you to hear it from me. I know that life hasn't been easy for you and if you feel the need to do this, then I won't stop you and neither will your aunt." Toby gave her a smile. "After all, you will always have a home to come back to. We will always be here for you."

Tilly let out a sob and threw her arms around the man who had given her security and stability, feeling him awkwardly pat her on the back. "Thank you. Thank you for everything."

He only held onto her for a moment longer before pulling back, clearing his throat. "Yes, well, eat your dinner and get a good night's rest. We have a full day tomorrow."

Tilly watched as Toby hurried out of her room, knowing that her show of affection had made him feel awkward.

The rest of the week went by in a blur and soon it was time for Tilly to depart. Her trunk was ready in the hallway when she took her last step from the stairs, saying goodbye to the twins first. "I will come and visit, I promise," she told them both, giving them each a hug. "I'm only a few streets away."

Neither said much and Tilly straightened, meeting her aunt's gaze. "I trust you have everything?" she said giving her a soft smile, looking at Tilly's packed case.

Tilly nodded, clasping her hands before her. "I believe I do."

"And you will come and visit?"

It wasn't as much of a question as it was a demand, but Tilly nodded all the same. "Of course, I will."

"Good," her aunt replied as Toby came into the house to gather Tilly's trunk. "It is time to go," he said, pecking his wife on the cheek dutifully. "I will be back soon enough."

Tilly drew in a breath before she decided that she would be the one to say a proper goodbye and embraced her aunt, feeling her stiffen slightly. "I know you think I'm making a mistake, but I have to be the one to make it."

"Oh, Matilda," her aunt sighed, returning her embrace. "I'm more afraid that I will never see you again."

Tilly's heart wrenched in her chest. "Please don't worry, I will come and visit regularly."

Her aunt let her go and took a few steps back, wiping her eyes as she did so. In all her years, Tilly had only seen her aunt cry once, long ago, and the sight now made her almost wish she hadn't made such a drastic decision. "I... I must go," she said instead, hurrying out of the house before her aunt could say another word.

Toby was waiting with the wagon and Tilly climbed up onto the front seat, keeping quiet as he clucked at the horses, sending them in motion. She wasn't making the wrong decision, but somehow, it felt as if maybe she was.

"I will look after her, do not worry yourself."

Tilly glanced at Toby, who was currently trying to navigate the horse through the crowded street. "I know you will. I just, I don't want her to be upset with me."

Toby sighed. "She's not upset. She's simply hurting, tis all."

Biting her lower lip, Tilly tried not to think about her aunt's feelings. Surely her aunt, of all people, would understand that Tilly needed to find her own way in life. It was a trait she had learnt from her father; she had his wandering spirit.

After all, he would have understood the need, though Tilly knew that her life would be far different if he had still been alive to this day.

Straightening her shoulders, Tilly forced herself to look forwards, not backwards. This was the right thing for her to do.

CHAPTER 8

The weeks went by at Tilly's new home. Orla, Mr Myers sixteen-year-old daughter, had proven to be the unconventional chaperone to Tilly. Orla was a giggly, sweet young woman, with a mass of blonde ringlets that framed her face and made her seem far younger than she actually was.

That and she talked about the silliest of things. Tilly was always grateful to escape to the shop in the mornings, spending her days making lovely floral arrangements that seemed to be snatched up in minutes, pleasing Mr Myers immensely.

Each evening, after a meagre supper that was usually provided by Orla's poor cooking skills, Tilly would watch the town from the second story window that faced the street. From the snug window seat, she could see some of the more well to do areas of London, watching as the gentlemen and graceful ladies walked to their destinations, dressed in fine evening attire.

There was an abundance of neatly painted coaches out and about everywhere in the evening, the shop was in a much better location to watch the comings and goings than her former home had been. Orla would sometimes join her, pointing out the ones that they recognised, such as the Duke of Bainbridge's coach or the famed Madame Dupont, who seemed to have a new suitor each evening.

Mostly, Tilly enjoyed her new found freedom away from her aunt and uncle, the solitude still more than enough even with Orla's girlish ways.

Tilly waited a few weeks before she decided to visit her aunt, taking her one day off to do so. She was dressed in a new gown purchased with her wages from Mr Myers, her crimson velvet bonnet tied under her chin set off nicely with a lovely blue satin bow. Truly, she felt as if she could be one of the women she saw from the window.

Her aunt took one look at her outfit and sniffed, holding the door open for her to come in. "Well, don't just stand there, child. Come on in."

The twins rushed to Tilly the moment she stepped over the threshold. "Why did you leave? We've missed you so," Hughie exclaimed, clinging to her legs.

"Don't you love us any longer?" Frank added, his soulful eyes reminding her of Toby.

"No, of course I love you, very much," she told them, pulling them both into her arms. "But I got a position in a flower shop, remember?"

Then they had remembered, and she spent an hour telling them about all the customers that had come into the shop, including the one gentleman who had brought his black dog with him. "Go on with you both," her aunt said after a while. "And wash up for dinner."

Tilly rose from the chair. "Can I help?"

Aunt Ruth shook her head. "I can manage just fine. After all, you are a guest here now."

Tilly bit her lower lip. "I don't wish to quarrel with you, Aunt Ruth. I was hoping that you might be happy for me."

Her aunt removed the spoon from the pot and turned to face her niece. "I wish I could say that I am happy for you, Matilda, but I don't see anything good coming from this at all. You are flirting with danger, being that close to the well to do gentry. What if one of them recognises you?"

Tilly let out a short laugh. "Then their memory is far better than mine. I was dressed as a boy then, remember? Besides, I was only young at the time. I am fully grown now."

"You still look like Matthew," her aunt said a moment later, her lips pursed. "Furthermore, you look like your father far too much now, Matilda. There could be a chance that someone could see you and think of him."

"Perhaps," Tilly admitted. She knew she looked a great deal like her father, but she also knew that it would be nigh on impossible for anyone to remember her. It had been so long ago, and the gossips had stopped talking a few months after her father's death. If someone were looking for her, wouldn't they have tracked down her aunt by now? "I'm safe, Aunt. I swear it."

"We will see," her aunt replied, turning back to the stove.

Tilly clasped her hands before her. "Mr Myers has said that I may be able to take over his shop one day." He had been pleased with her work so far and she had the business sense that his daughter did not. Foolish Orla was already plotting on snagging herself a wealthy London gentleman to look after her in her future years.

Aunt Ruth sniffed and Tilly's shoulders sagged. It mattered not that she was trying to secure her own future. Her aunt would never be pleased with what she was doing.

However, Aunt Ruth's fears did come true a just few weeks later, as Tilly was helping a servant with a rather large purchase. "He's having a party," the servant named Ursula stated as she hefted a heavy bundle of gorgeously scented flowers in her arms. "It is tonight, of course. We have been working all week to get the house ready."

"Then by all means let me carry these out for you," Tilly offered, seeing the exhaustion on the young woman's face.

Ursula smiled and together they walked out into the London sunshine, the sights and smells of London all around them. A shiny black coach waited by the curb, the matching black horses stomping on the cobblestone street. "He's in there," Ursula stated in a soft voice as the footman opened the door for them.

Tilly stood politely waiting until Ursula had placed her floral display in the coach before moving out of the way so that Tilly could do the same. When she raised her eyes, she found herself staring into the ageing face of Lord Farthing.

Oh no…

His eyes widened but Tilly was already hurrying away, glad to see that Ursula had cajoled the footman into helping her. "Wait," she heard him call out behind her, but she was already moving back into the shop, picking up her skirts to enable her to move quicker.

Mr Myers was coming out of the back room when she entered. "What's wrong?" he asked, noting her flushed cheeks.

"I... I don't feel so well," Tilly lied. "I need to lie down upstairs."

"Of course," the older man stated kindly with a nod. "You've been working too hard lately. Take a break, Tilly."

She ducked her head and hurried up the stairs, finding Orla lying across her small, narrow bed pretending to read her latest novella. "What's wrong with you?" Orla asked as Tilly hurried to the window, peering out. To her relief, Lord Farthing's coach was pulling away from the curb, taking the man further down the street and out of sight.

He wasn't coming for her. "Oh, nothing, I just feel a little light-headed," she stated, pushing away from the window to lie on her bed. Drawing in deep breaths, Tilly forced herself to relax. He didn't know who she was.

He couldn't.

The last thing she wanted to see was the man who quite possibly was responsible for killing her father. Lord Farthing was the last person to see him alive and Tilly didn't believe for one moment that her father had taken his own life. He wouldn't leave her, not as he had. He had doted on her.

Lord Farthing had discovered the ploy that her father had set up with Tilly pretending to be a boy and their lives were all but ruined as soon as he found out the truth.

Lord Farthing had ruined them.

A tear leaked out of the corner of her eye, and she wiped it away before Orla could see. The last thing she wanted to do was explain her sad past to the young woman.

The afternoon stretched into evening and when the lamp was lit in the room, Tilly found Orla cracking open the window before pressing herself into the drapes. "Whatever are you doing?" she asked, sitting up on the bed, pushing her now haphazard hair out of her face.

The young girl blushed. "Shh! He will be here soon."

He? Tilly climbed off the bed and walked over to the window, noting that the streets were starting to empty due to the lateness of the hour. "Do you have a suitor, Orla?"

Orla shook her head, her ringlets dancing about her face. "Nay but I find myself eager to look out for him. I… I can't even talk to him. I am so tongue-tied."

"You should just be yourself," Tilly said, clasping her hands before her. She had never been besotted with a boy in her life, but if she had learnt anything from her father's situation, it was to be honest and truthful with everyone that she met.

Except, perhaps, Lord Farthing, that was. "Who is he?"

"He's the lamplighter," Orla said softly, her bright blue eyes darting to the window. "Oh, Tilly! He's perhaps the most handsome man I've ever seen!"

Tilly swallowed her laughter. "Well, then you must talk to him when he arrives."

"Oh!" Orla gasped. "Here he comes!"

Tilly followed the young woman to the window and watched as a tall gentleman with copper-coloured hair walked down the street, a long-wicked pole in one hand, and whistling a cheery tune. From their vantage point, she couldn't make out his features, but he lit one lamp after another, stopping at their home to peer up at the window. "Good evening!" he called out, tipping his face up to them.

Tilly nudged Orla in the ribs. "Good...good evening!" the young woman called out, followed by a childish giggle.

He proceeded to light their lamp, the flare of orange flame illuminating the building and brightening his hair further. "You won't believe what I have seen tonight," he continued in a sing-song voice as he pulled the wick away. "There's a right large ball going on tonight, with coaches and carriages lined up along the street. The coaches are carrying ladies and gents in all their finery."

Orla let out a giggle as Tilly leant against the windowsill, wanting to hear more. It was the life that her father had introduced her to all those years ago, the very lifestyle that Lord Farthing belonged to. What she wouldn't give to take a turn about the ballroom, dressed in a beautiful gown, laughing at something her dance partner had whispered in her ear as the music played on.

Oh, to be able to play chess again in a room full of patrons, the whispers all about the moves she was making and their rapt attention on nothing more than herself.

"And you, who are you?" the man questioned.

Tilly snapped out of her thoughts. "Oh, she's new," Orla supplied for Tilly, smiling at the lamplighter. "She works for my father."

"Aye, I do," Tilly added, lifting her chin. She was proud of the fact that she had procured a good position, carving out a future that her father would have been proud of considering she wasn't able to play chess any longer.

"Well, now," he replied, tipping his head back. He was definitely nearer to Tilly's age, perhaps a few years older, and she was taken aback by his cheerful smile, one that seemed to light up his entire face. "I never thought that Old Man Myers would replace his lovely daughter."

"She hasn't replaced me, silly," Orla said quickly, suddenly finding her voice. "She helps my papa in the shop."

Tilly didn't take offence at her choice of words. She was, after all, hired help.

"And your name is?" he asked hopefully, his eyes shining on Tilly.

"Not before yours," she challenged, all thoughts of Lord Farthing vanishing.

He chuckled and Tilly's stomach warmed at the sound. "Emrys," he called out. "Emrys, the lamplighter."

"Tilly," she answered, leaning out of the window. "Tilly, the flower arranger."

His smile was wide. "Until we meet again then, Tilly."

Tilly watched as he moved down the street to the next lamp and when she pulled herself back into the window, Orla was there, a frown clouding her face. "I hope you don't think that he's interested in you," she said in a huff.

"Of course, not," Tilly snorted, walking over to her bed. "I have no interest in him whatsoever."

"Good," Orla replied falling onto her bed. "Because I took a fancy to him first."

Tilly didn't respond, instead turning to face the wall, a smile playing on her lips. Emrys. What a peculiar name.

CHAPTER 9

"What do you think is the most exciting thing about your position?"

Tilly watched from her perch in the window as Emrys thought over her question, clearly thinking thoroughly. "I suppose the threat of setting something on fire, but I don't think my boss would be very impressed."

Tilly laughed. "I think you might be right, at that!"

Emrys chuckled, leaning against the very lamp he had just lit so that they could see one another more clearly.

She smiled down at him, wishing she could see him up close. Every evening for the past five nights, they had carried on a conversation much like this, learning snippets about each other that would carry Tilly through to the next evening, when she knew he would come by. Orla had all but given up on even joining in on their conversations now, pretending to be asleep when Tilly knew that she listened in on every word they said. Deep down, Tilly knew that Emrys would never be suitable for Orla, he was never going to be the wealthy gentleman that she so desired.

Tilly couldn't help that Emrys had asked for her on the second night and the third, nor that she looked forward to their conversations. He was truly her first friend in London, though she wouldn't dare go as far to say it was a courtship.

After all, it had only been five nights.

"Tell me, Tilly," Emrys was saying, his hands in his pockets. "What would you say if I asked you something right proper?"

"It depends on what it was," Tilly responded, her heart speeding up. "And I didn't know you had a proper bone in your body, Emrys."

He chuckled, her favourite sound, as of late. There were many things that Tilly found herself fond of about the young man. "Aye, I do on occasion. Would you do me the honour of coming for a walk with me?"

Tilly held her hand up to her throat nervously. "We cannot, not at night." There was her reputation to consider and since Mr Myers prided himself on her modest ways, she couldn't possibly disappoint him. She liked her position far too much.

Emrys pressed his hand to his chest in mock horror. "You wound me, my fair Tilly, if you thought I would make such an improper gesture!"

Tilly smiled at his jest. Emrys could always make her smile whenever she was feeling poorly about something. He was never anything but jovial. "Then what could you have possibly meant?"

Emrys pulled off his cap, holding it in his hands. "I would like to come and meet you outside the shop tomorrow, during the day, when you are on your break, then we would have no need for a chaperone. Perhaps I could introduce you to one of Mr Johnson's meat pies?"

Tilly knew she should say no. She needed to focus on her work, on making certain that she gave Mr Myers no reason to let her go and force her back to her aunt's home.

But the lure was far too tempting. To spend time outside, with Emrys, would feel good…or maybe it wouldn't.

There was only one way to find out. "Yes," she answered as she removed herself from the windowsill. "I will wait upon your arrival tomorrow lunchtime."

Emrys bowed with a flourish, as if he was a genteel gentleman. "Then I bid you good night, my dear lady Tilly. Until we meet once more."

Tilly closed the window and turned to the room, finding Orla glaring at her. "You shouldn't tease him so," Orla replied, her arms crossed over her generous bosom. "You have no interest in him. Not like I do."

Tilly walked over to her own bed, unlacing her boots. "Your father would never allow him to court you. He wants you to find one of those fine gentlemen." Mr Myers had expressed that sentiment more than once during their work, wanting Orla to have all the fine things in life that he could never provide, even though he was a successful businessman in his own right.

Orla continued to frown, some of the anger leaving her expression. "Perhaps, but I want Emrys."

"Our conversations mean nothing," Tilly murmured as she changed from her dress to her nightgown. Even the words didn't feel right on her tongue, and she knew that she was not only lying to Orla, but also to herself.

"I heard you," Orla stated as Tilly pulled the covers back on the bed. "I heard that catch in your voice, Tilly. You are infatuated with him."

Tilly climbed into the cool sheets and turned to face Orla. "Perhaps I just like someone who can make me laugh."

Orla huffed but Tilly was already turning away, suddenly tired of the conversation. Emrys…she didn't know how to explain him to anyone, but he made her feel, well, special. He made her forget about the tragedies in her past and she knew something was growing inside of her that could be special between them.

Or it could just be a fleeting fantasy. Either way, she was hoping that he was going to be at the shop at the appointed time, regardless.

The next morning, Tilly decided to approach Mr Myers about Emrys, telling him about the proposition for a noon time walk down the street. "Aye, I know of the lad," Mr Myers stated as he gave some red roses and lilies to Tilly to arrange. "Good lad with an acceptable position. You could do much worse, Tilly. I think it would be good for you to get out of the shop, to meet those of your own age."

Tilly drew in a breath. "Orla, she has her eyes set on him herself."

Mr Myers chuckled. "As she did the one before Emrys? Pay my daughter no mind, Tilly. She has fanciful notions about all the gentlemen that may give her a passing glance." He shook his head, a frown marring his normally kind face. "She has too much of her mama in her, I'm afraid. She left shortly after Orla was born, leaving me with a babe to care for."

Tilly's heart went out to the kind man. "I'm sorry. You have done well in raising her."

He eyed her, a wry smile crossing his lips. "Aye, I have. Have a care with Emrys, Tilly. He might be a good lad, but he also has a silver tongue."

Tilly laughed and went about her day, feeling her heart start to pound in her ears as noon approached. Perhaps he was just jesting her and wouldn't come. She would be hurt of course, but at least he would no longer be a distraction to her.

Just before noon, the door opened and Emrys walked in, his cocky smile causing Tilly's heart to speed up. "Tilly?" he asked, letting out a low whistle. "You are far lovelier than you appear in the window."

He was far more handsome too. With his cap off, his wavy auburn hair was unfashionably long, his hazel eyes full of laughter. He was lean but strong and his clothing was neatly pressed. "And you seem taller," she countered, drawing a laugh from him.

Emrys proffered an arm. "Shall we, Tilly?"

Tilly felt her cheeks warm as she slid her arm in his, letting her hand rest on his strong forearm. "Lead me to the meat pies."

They exited the shop and started down the street, crowded with vendors selling their wares and patrons purchasing them. "Tell me about yourself," she told him lightly, enjoying the way he manoeuvred through the throng of people, always careful to tug her along.

He grinned. "There's not much to say that you don't already know, Tilly."

"Surely there's something," she urged.

He looked out into the distance, his expression growing pensive. "My family are from Wales. I rent a room not far from here and send funds back when I can to my Mam."

"You miss her," she said, hearing the longing in his voice.

His eyes met hers. "Aye, I do. My youngest brother, Gwilym, is learning to be a blacksmith back home and he sends me reminders of home." Tilly watched as he reached into the pocket of his trousers, pulling out a small iron forged flower. "For you."

"Oh, I couldn't possibly!" she said as he tried to hand it to her. "It's yours."

"It's mine until I deem it someone else's," Emrys pressed. "Now, I want you to have it. Gwilym, he would be pleased to know I have finally given it to a lovely lass."

With her cheeks burning, Tilly accepted the small flower, tracing the firm petals with her finger. "Please tell him thank you. It is lovely."

Her companion cleared his throat and they moved on, toward the meat pies that he had promised her. "Tell me of your hopes," he said casually. "Surely a lass like you has hopes and dreams."

"Aye, I do." Tilly sighed, thinking of the flower shop and the changes she would make once Mr Myers wasn't there to manage it. "I wish to own my own flower shop, to do my arrangements and bouquets."

"And what else do you dream about?" Emrys pressed as they joined the queue for the pies. "Surely there's more."

It was on the tip of her tongue to tell him about her chess playing but she held back. That wasn't who she was any longer. She was a florist. "I'm afraid that is it."

Emrys tightened his hold on her arm. "Well, then, that's enough. Look at us! A leerie and a flower girl!

It is not going to house us in Mayfair, but it will keep food in our bellies!"

Tilly smiled as they stepped forward to pay for their pies, taking the crusty shells to the small park not far from the vendor, a park she had spied from the shop window. They found a small stone wall to sit upon and Tilly took a bite, the flavours bursting on her tongue. "Oh!"

"The best meat pies in all of London," Emrys announced. "Even some of the fine folks at times send their servants to buy them. I hear that even the queen herself has asked for a delivery."

Tilly tried to picture the queen purchasing a meat pie and laughed, earning a smile from Emrys. "You have a right lovely laugh," he murmured, lifting his pie to his mouth.

Flustered, Tilly did the same, busying herself with eating the flaky wonder. Once she had taken the last bite, she sighed. "That was wonderful."

"Aye, it was," Emrys replied, wiping his hands on his trousers. "And much better since you were with me today."

"You are a true flatterer," Tilly accused with a smile. "I bet I am not the only girl you have taken to this place and plied with meat pies."

Emrys gave her a genuine smile. "Aye, you are lass. I confess, I tend to run my mouth a good bit of the time, but this is my first time walking out with someone."

Tilly was flattered, truly. As she watched Emrys, she realised that she had enjoyed his company very much and not because he had bought her a meat pie. It was his laughter, his wide smile, the way he made her feel.

She enjoyed it all.

"Well," he was saying, standing to extend his hand toward her. "I best get you back."

Tilly accepted his hand but as he pulled her to her feet, she stumbled and felt herself falling toward him. In a flash, Emrys had her cradled against him, their bodies touching from head to toe.

It felt, well, it felt lovely. "Oh!" she exclaimed, staring up at him. "I'm so sorry."

He released her slowly, tipping her chin with his finger. "If I didn't know any better, Tilly, I would think you did that on purpose."

Tilly stammered but Emrys just winked at her, proffering his arm. "Come now. I'm just jesting with you. Let me see you home."

When they arrived back at the flower shop, Emrys let go of her arm, lifting her hand to his lips instead, lightly brushing her knuckles. "Until tonight, fair Tilly."

"What makes you think that I will be there?" she asked breathlessly, feeling his touch all the way to her very soul.

Emrys dropped her hand and straightened, tucking his hands in his pockets. "Because you won't be able to stay away."

Tilly watched him walk away, his cheery tune still heard over the din of the crowd and sighed happily. What a perfect encounter with Emrys!

"Well, now, I see it went well."

Turning, she found Mr Myers grinning from the doorway, the ever-present broom in his hand. "How do you know?"

"Because," he stated as he swept the already clean doorstep, "the look on your face is one of pure infatuation."

Tilly's cheeks burned but she knew that he was right. She could have spent the entire day in Emrys's company and never tired of his smile, his jesting, the way he had brushed his lips over her hand. What would they feel like against her own lips?

"Come, now," Mr Myers chuckled. "It is time to get back to work, Tilly. Oh, by the way, there is a letter for you. I put it on the counter."

Curious, Tilly walked inside the shop and picked up the missive. Who would be sending her a letter and here of all places? Surely not her aunt as she visited regularly.

Breaking the seal open, she pulled out a single piece of vellum, opening it with a gasp.

You may be moving up in the world, it started. *But you will always be Little Matthew to me.*

Someone had recognised her.

CHAPTER 10

Tilly had to wait until her next day off before she could show her aunt the letter, pulling it out of her small bag the moment she crossed the threshold. "You were right," she panted. "Someone knows."

Her aunt took the letter and read its contents, clucking her tongue. "I tried to warn you, Matilda. Now look what you have done."

Tilly fell into the chair at the table, miserable. She hadn't slept much since receiving the note, waiting for the moment that all of London would know what she had done as a small child.

"You drew too much attention to yourself," her aunt chided, handing the note back to her niece, a frown on her face. "Perhaps it is time for you to come home. Toby and I can protect you best here."

Tilly looked around the small home. This wasn't her home. Her small room, even with Orla in it, was her home now. She enjoyed taking care of the customers and helping out Mr Myers. She enjoyed the work she did with her hands, and to see the excitement on the customer's faces when they picked up her creations.

Most of all, she enjoyed her time with Emrys. If she moved back here, she would lose him and suddenly her heart wrenched at the thought. There would be no more window meetings or laughing at his silly jokes. She would no longer get to see his hazel eyes roam over her face or feel the warmth in his gaze.

No, she couldn't allow herself to give that up. She had just found him. "I can't," she forced out. "I can't come home."

Aunt Ruth eyed her, clear disapproval on her face. "So, you are going to take a chance? That doesn't sound very smart, Matilda."

Tilly pushed herself out of the chair, setting her jaw. "I can't just give up now. I am enjoying my work and my life, Aunt Ruth. I've made friends, I… I even have an admirer. I'm not willing to give any of that up."

"Then you are selfish," her aunt shot back before sighing. "Listen, I don't want you hurt Matilda, but you are set on doing so yourself. Think of the shame. Think of the hurt that you had before. This is a sign!"

Tilly strode to the door, her heart and her head hurting. "I can't give up, Aunt Ruth. Papa would want me to fight."

"Your father didn't fight for you."

Gasping Tilly felt the brunt of her aunt's harsh words, not saying another word as she left her old home, crying all the way back to the shop. She didn't like quarrelling with her aunt, but Aunt Ruth couldn't possibly understand what happiness Tilly had found by doing this. It was one note and not at all threatening in the least.

Although her aunt had been right on one account. Her father had never fought for her, instead he had used her for his own ill-gotten gains.

Unfortunately, the letter was not the end of her plight. Over the next few weeks, Tilly continued to receive notes from an unseen person, detailing the shame that her father had brought upon their family by pretending she was something she wasn't. Some were short, while others were a little longer, but they all had the same threatening undertone.

So much so that on one of her lunch break walks with Emrys, Tilly could have sworn someone was following them. "There!" she shouted, pointing at a tall gentleman a few feet away. "He's following us."

"Tilly," Emrys said softly, gathering her hands in his. "He's not following us. What is going on with you? Why have you been so scared recently?"

She looked into the concerned eyes of the man who had brought her joy. She couldn't possibly drag him into her life right now, not when he could be hurt— and if Emrys got hurt, Tilly would never forgive herself. He meant that much to her. "I simply can't tell you."

"Can't or won't?" he asked lightly, ire flooding his expression. "You've been like this for weeks now and I can't help you unless you tell me."

"I don't want to tell you!" she cried, pulling her hands from his. "There's nothing you can do, Emrys, nothing at all." It was her burden to bear and hers alone.

"Please," he said, reaching for her again. "Please let me help, Tilly."

Tears threatened her eyes. He was trying to help, she knew that, but he couldn't possibly help her. If she told him what she had done, what her father had made her do, he would hate her as well. "Let it go, Emrys," she said coolly. If he wouldn't listen to her pleading, then she would have to make sure that he understood she wasn't going to tell him.

"Nay," he continued, grabbing at her hands once more. "I love you, Tilly."

Tilly's world tilted and she stumbled back with a gasp. "What?" This could not be happening right now!

His normally teasing countenance was serious now, his eyes on hers. "I love you. I think I have for a long time but..." He chuckled, a hint of a smile on his face. "Well, I didn't plan on saying it like this but there you have it. I love you."

As much as her heart leapt into her throat, Tilly couldn't enjoy the moment. "I... I can't do this right now," she said in a hurry, turning and walking away before he could see her tears. She could hear him shouting her name behind her, but Tilly refused to turn around, no matter how much she wished to. Emrys loved her. As much as she wanted to have him hold her tightly and never let go, the threat of someone coming after her was real and she couldn't put him in that sort of danger.

She wasn't even worried about their brief time together. She truly did care for him, perhaps she even loved him as well.

It wasn't the only thing she had to worry about. A few days later, after Tilly had avoided Emrys nearly every night, even taking her breaks in her room so that he wouldn't see her, Mr Myers asked for her to join him one evening in the shop. "You wanted to see me?" she asked as she joined him at the table.

"Aye," he stated, a book before him. "I'm re-writing my Will and I want to know if you would like to have the shop after I am gone."

Tilly could hardly breathe. He wanted to leave her the flower shop? "I... I don't know what to say," she said slowly.

He smiled, picking up his ink pen and dipping it in the well. "There will be some requests of course. If necessary, Orla will need to be provided for until she is wed and no contracts that I list will have their prices raised just because I am gone."

"Why me?" she asked hesitantly. She was nothing more than a girl who had listened well and read books to gain her trade.

Mr Myers eyed her. "Because you are a bright, capable woman, without a hint of scandal to your name. You have made a name for yourself, Tilly, and you should be rewarded for what you have done. If I leave the shop in your name, I feel certain you will do what is best for it and for the future."

It was what she had hoped for when she had joined Mr Myers, to one day take over the shop and continue to provide lovely arrangements for their customers.

Now that she was receiving the anonymous communications, she couldn't accept it, not at this moment. "I need to think about it," she told him.

He arched a brow. "Think on what? Wasn't this your dream all along?"

"It's happening too fast," she said in a rush. First Emrys professing his love for her and now this. It was everything she could have wanted for her life, yet she couldn't enjoy any of it. "I need a few days to think on what you have said."

He placed the pen on the book, giving her a kind smile. "Of course. I apologise. You are right. This shouldn't be taken lightly."

Tilly nodded and escaped to her room, glad to see that Orla was already asleep, her gentle snores filling the air. Numb to her feelings, she climbed into bed, allowing the tears to stream down her cheeks and wet the pillow beneath. How could everything start to go well in her life yet fall apart at the same time?

The next evening, as Tilly was helping Mr Myers close the shop for the night, another letter was delivered with her name on it. "You must have an admirer," Mr Myers remarked as he handed her the letter. "You have received a fair few of these lately."

She gave him a faint smile, excusing herself to read the contents in private, her hands shaking as she broke the seal. It would have been a grand wish to think that the letter came from an admirer, or her aunt, but in her heart, Tilly knew who it was truly from.

Your secret past will be told everywhere two days from now unless you disappear once more.

Tilly pressed her hand to her mouth to hold back the sob, tucking the letter in the pocket of her apron with her other hand. Until now she felt that perhaps if she ignored the threats, they would eventually grow tired of their fun and leave her alone.

This, this was quite serious.

Pressing her head against the wall under the stairs, she tried to contemplate her options. As much as she didn't want to leave the shop, she couldn't very well attach a scandal to Mr Myers or to Orla. He had accepted that she was a fine upstanding lady, one that had come because she wanted something more in her life and not because she was running from her past.

She hadn't been, until the letters had started, that much was true.

Now, if she stayed, she would be putting them through something that was not their fault, something that they had no concern over. It was her own fault that she thought she could have more than a life with her aunt!

Pushing away from the wall, Tilly fought the tears as she climbed the stairs, knowing what she must do. There was nothing else she could do to stop this except leave and go back to her aunt's. Aunt Ruth would know how to deal with this matter and if she had to hide there for a while, then she would.

Orla wasn't in her bed as Tilly entered the bedroom and quickly, she packed her belongings into a small carpet bag instead of her trunk, leaving behind many of her things. Perhaps she could send Toby to retrieve them later.

Darkness started to creep into the room and Tilly fought and failed not to move to the window, waiting for the moment that Emrys would come down the street, his cheery tune filling the night air. She thought back to his words, how they had filled her with joy once she realised that he had in fact told her that he loved her and wished she had reacted differently to them. They were the words every young woman wanted to hear but the concern was that Emrys didn't know who she truly was.

It didn't matter, Tilly told herself as she saw the faint glow of the Leerie's light in the distance. She couldn't very well tell Emrys how she felt and move promptly back into her aunt's household, now could she?

Nor would she want him to potentially be in danger because he had associated himself with her, not knowing what she had done in her past, even though she had been but a young child under her father's direction.

What would he say? Tilly liked to think that he wouldn't be worried that much by her past. After all, it wasn't as if she had been a fallen woman of ill repute, but she had lied. She had duped some powerful gentlemen in London, some of whom quite possibly had figured out who she was.

Emrys drew near and Tilly pressed her face to the glass, wanting one last glimpse of her love before she had to leave him forever. Would he pine for her? She didn't want him to do so. She wanted him to move forward, to find a woman who didn't have her past.

She wanted him to love someone else, no matter how terrible it felt to think that way.

But as the leerie drew closer, Tilly realised it wasn't Emrys at all, but an older gentleman with greying hair, shuffling his way down the dirtied pavement. Despair and concern threaded through her as she turned away from the window, looking at her bed and the bag upon it. Did Emrys not wish to see her any longer.

Not that she could blame him. He probably thought she had spurned him, but if the truth came out, she knew that he would be grateful she had.

CHAPTER 11

When dawn crept over the horizon, Tilly gathered her belongings quietly and stole down the stairs and out the front door, grateful that Mr Myers wasn't already in the shop as she did so. She had left a note explaining her need to leave them so that they wouldn't face further shame but didn't go into detail about her own scandal for fear that they might come after her. She also told the shopkeeper that she was grateful for the opportunity he had provided for her and that she was sorry that she couldn't carry on his legacy.

Tilly had written the words with tears in her eyes, wishing that her situation was different, but it wasn't and now she was left to handle the scandal that her father had started. Now that she was a grown woman, she could see how her father had tricked them all, including her. He had made it seem as if it was all in good fun, dressing her up as a boy and having her play chess, but he had won money for their charade.

Now there was nothing exciting about her previous life. If only he could see what she was doing now, how she was attempting to move on with her life but couldn't, not with the scandal hanging over her head.

Mr Myers deserved to give his shop, his legacy, to someone he could count on, someone who wasn't going to lie to him as Tilly had.

Hurrying in the direction of her aunt's home, Tilly nearly bowled over Emrys, who was finishing extinguishing the lamps near their home. "Tilly?" he asked as she tried to brush past him. "Wait!"

"I can't talk to you," she mumbled, clutching her bag a little tighter. If she did, she might just cry and right now, she was trying to do her very best to hold herself together.

"Yes, you can," he stated firmly, grasping her elbow and forcing Tilly to face him.

Tilly saw the dark circles under his eyes that matched her own, his normal jovial expression withdrawn, and felt miserable at what she had done to him. "Emrys, I…"

He shook his head, keeping a firm grip on her elbow. "Let me escort you to wherever you are going," he replied, his eyes flickering to the bag in her hands. "Before you go disappearing on me completely."

Tilly knew she should deny him, but she couldn't, her heart crying out at the feelings she had for him, and how they had ended up. No, how *she* had ended things between them. "I'm sorry," she rushed out, pushing her tears back. "I didn't mean to hurt you. I… I've been looking for you at the window every night and you didn't come by, and I thought the worst."

He pressed his finger to her lips, silencing her. "I know and I thought we both needed some time apart. I took another lighting route so that I could think clearly."

"You can't think clearly around me?" she asked as he removed his finger.

His lips lifted in a smile, but it never reached his eyes. "No, I can't. I wish that you would let me help you, Tilly." Emrys let out a breath. "I know you didn't mean to hurt me. Something has frightened you and I want to know what it is. I want to help, Tilly. I... I care about you, and I don't want to lose you."

She turned to face him, seeing both the concern and tenderness in his gaze. "I don't want to lose you either," she said softly.

He gave her a hesitant smile. "Then walk with me and let's figure this out."

They set out in the direction she had been heading, and Tilly proceeded to tell Emrys all about her former life, how her father had found the talent within Tilly and decided to exploit it, fooling most of London while he did so. She told him of the captain's death and how she suspected that he didn't actually kill himself but that whoever was blackmailing him had a hand in it.

Street after street they walked, slowly, with Emrys's comforting hand on her elbow, until she had run out of words to say. "That's all," she stated, feeling drained for even talking about it. "That's everything."

Emrys cleared his throat. "I… I really don't know what to say," he replied, clearly taken aback by everything she had said. "I mean, you are a chess prodigy, Tilly! That's most extraordinary!"

Her cheeks flushed at his sudden praise, but it mattered not. It didn't stop the fact that someone was threatening to expose everything, and she couldn't go through with that. She couldn't let her family go through it. "It still doesn't help me." She would never pick up another chess piece if this would all go away, and she could have a normal life with Emrys and work in the flower shop for the rest of her days. She didn't even need to own it.

Emrys scratched his chin. "Perhaps not but I think that you shouldn't be ashamed of your abilities. It doesn't matter if you are a woman or a man as long as you can prove your worth." His eyes lightened. "I want you to prove your ability to me."

Tilly glanced ahead, seeing the street on which her aunt's home was on. She shouldn't. It would bring nothing but pain and solve nothing. She hadn't played chess since the day they had come to London all those years ago, unable to have herself relive the pain of what the game had brought to her.

"We can find a chess set," Emrys was saying, looking around. "Surely, I can procure one."

Tilly bit her lip. "There's no need," she replied, opening her bag. It was the one thing she hadn't been able to leave behind, the last remaining gift she had received from her father. Reaching in, she pulled out the flat wooden box. "I already have a set."

Emrys let out a low whistle as he eyed the small wooden box, the polished wood gleaming in the morning sun. "You are taking this very seriously, Tilly." He grabbed her hand and Tilly couldn't help but shiver at his touch. It had been far too long since she had seen him, and Tilly realised she would have been missing a piece of herself if she had remained away from Emrys. He clearly didn't mind at all the trouble that she had been in and seemed to want to help her instead.

It warmed her heart.

Emrys led her over to Battersea Park, a place she knew like the back of her hand, and to a bench that was wide enough for both of them to sit upon. "Have you ever played?" she asked curiously, placing the box on the bench and opening the little drawers that held the pieces. They had talked about a lot of things, but this was not one of them.

It was his turn to blush as he set out the pieces. "My grandmother demanded that I learn some finer qualities of being a gentleman to try and impress the gentry if such a time arose." He chuckled. "I'm not certain how my chess abilities were supposed to help, but yet here we are."

Maybe it was fate that had brought them together after all. "Let's see how well you remember," Tilly challenged, the old memories of how she would conquer her opponents soundly welling up inside. While she enjoyed arranging flowers and making their patrons happy, chess was truly where she had felt accomplished, the rush of excitement hard to contain as Emrys made the first move. "Take it easy on me, my love," he replied, some of the light returning in his eyes.

Tilly didn't however and in a matter of minutes, she had defeated him. "You're jesting," Emrys replied, shock on his handsome face. "Tilly, my love, that was simply remarkable."

"It was simple, really," she explained, showing him where he had made the moves allowing her to take the game.

Emrys chuckled as he helped her reset the board. "In another time, I might be quite perturbed that you just beat me, but seeing that spark in your eye, it is all worth the pain."

A laugh escaped Tilly and she suddenly felt lighter, having played for the first time in years, perhaps since her father had died. "Again," Emrys urged, giving her a wink.

So, they did. The early morning fog burned off and the sun rose high in the sky above them while Emrys and Tilly played game after game, Tilly winning soundly each time.

She had thought that Emrys would grow angered after the first few games, but he would only chuckle and urge her to show him where he had failed. It wasn't long before the park started to become busy with the morning foot traffic and they started to attract some attention. Tilly heard the whispers, the gasps when she beat Emrys, but he only urged her to continue, charming the crowd with his wit and humour.

"She's quite the player," one gentleman remarked, his hands clasped behind his back as he watched Tilly make a move.

"Aye," Emrys called out, winking at Tilly. "And she's mine."

Tilly laughed and they started again, playing well after midday. When her stomach started to grumble, Emrys declared a truce. "While I enjoy you soundly beating me game after game," he stated as they gathered the pieces and the crowd dispersed. "I feel as if I have to pull a scrap of my pride back."

Putting the pieces in the small drawers and closing the board, Tilly placed it lovingly back into her bag. "You did ask for those games."

"So, I did," Emrys said, standing. He reached his hand out and she accepted it, allowing him to pull her to her feet. "I just didn't think I would get beaten so soundly." He tucked her hand into the crook of his arm and guided her toward the street that her aunt's home resided on. "How do you feel?"

Tilly drew in a breath. She felt, well she felt as if she had found a new part of herself that had been buried long ago. The good news was that her skills hadn't been just when she was disguised as Matthew, but truly hers and hers alone. With some more practice, Tilly could bring back all her moves from her past if she wanted.

But what would be the reason for her to continue? Aside from Emrys, Tilly had no plans to step back into the spotlight with her playing abilities and, given the threatening notes she had been receiving, she couldn't.

Even if her heart enjoyed the game.

They finally arrived at her aunt's home and Emrys handed her the bag he had carried for her from the park. "Well, please tell me that you aren't going to run from this home in the next few days," he murmured, tucking a stray lock of hair behind her ear.

"Why do you want to know?"

"Because" he leaned closer, the smell of lamp oil clinging to his clothes. "I need to know where to come and properly propose to my love."

Tilly's heart fluttered but she had no time to react before Emrys was brushing his lips over hers.

Her first kiss. Tilly felt the same warmth creep into her bones, the feeling of rightness settling in her soul. Emrys pulled back. "Too forward?" he murmured, his hands on her upper arms.

"Not enough," she admitted with a small smile, her lips still tingling where his had been.

"So, you will marry me?" he asked hopefully.

Tilly stared into his lovely warm eyes, knowing that she wouldn't want anything less than to be Emrys's wife. He had taken her secret and helped her flourish it instead of running away and that meant everything to Tilly. "I can't give you an answer right this minute," she said instead, watching as his shoulders fell. "I have to find out what to do about the threat." She couldn't wed him without closing that chapter of her life. Only then would she know that she could step into her future with him. "But," Tilly continued, bringing her hand up to touch his cheek lovingly, "the answer will be yes whenever I am able to."

"You are going to torture me," Emrys groaned, leaning into her touch. "I never thought you would be so cruel."

Tilly gave him a soft smile, stepping back. "I have things that require my attention first."

"Of course, you do, my love," Emrys said, bowing over her hand. "And know that I'm not going anywhere. If you need me, you can always call on me."

She felt the barest brush of his lips on her knuckles before he was heading down the pavement, a cheery tune filling the air. Tilly had never considered falling in love, but Emrys had shown her that she didn't have to plan it, that her heart knew what it wanted, and she wanted a future with him.

With a sigh, Tilly forced her thoughts to the real reason she was back here at her aunt's home. She couldn't very well have a future until she laid her past to rest.

CHAPTER 12

When Tilly entered the home, she found Toby at the kitchen table, instead of her aunt, a steaming cup of tea before him. "Tilly," he said, surprised to see her. "What are you doing here?"

Tilly closed the door behind her and set her bag on the floor. The house was silent, unlike the constant buzz of conversation that she was used to in the flower shop, and Tilly's heart constricted as she thought about the very place that had given her so much joy in her life. "Where is Aunt Ruth?"

Toby sighed, looking more exhausted than usual. "The twins have colds. She was up half the night tending to them. I imagine she is in bed or at least I hope she is."

Inwardly sighing, Tilly knew that she couldn't very well bother her aunt now about her own troubles. She was home now, just as the letter had all but told her to do, and unless she set foot near the flower shop again, she might be safe.

Tilly may be able to protect them all by following their demands. If it were Lord Farthing, he would have a devil of a time attempting to find her. Mr Myers wasn't aware of where Tilly lived and Emrys wouldn't open his mouth now that he knew why Tilly had run.

"Is something amiss?" Toby asked.

Tilly wished to tell him, but it would only cause him grief. Her aunt was the only one that might understand what was going on, and what Tilly needed to do. After all, she wished to have a future, one with a certain Leerie, as soon as possible. "Nothing that can't wait," Tilly replied, clasping her hands before her. After her morning with Emrys, she had a new outlook on her life, and hoped that it would be in her future as well. "Are you finishing your lunch break?"

"Aye," Toby replied before draining his cup and standing. "I am heading back to the park to tend to some of the beds." He eyed her bland gown. "You wouldn't like to join me, would you?"

Tilly looked around the quiet home. If she couldn't talk to her aunt, then there was nothing else for her to do but wait. At least she could have her hands full, in some fertile soil, carefully picking the dead heads off the flowers while she waited. "I would enjoy that, thank you."

He nodded and after a few moments, they headed to the same park that she had been at earlier. Just as before, Tilly and Toby fell into a companionable silence, working alongside each other, and Tilly started to feel the tension ease from her shoulders.

"Why did you come back?" Toby asked after nearly an hour of work. "Tell me, what is amiss, Tilly."

Tilly sighed, her fingers dark with soil. She wished to discuss it with her aunt first, but Toby had always been a good listener and had given her sound advice whenever she had needed it.

She told him of the letters, how they had become more threatening over time and how she had no other choice but to leave the flower shop or else risk being exposed for what her father had done so many years ago. "They told me that they would expose me in two days' time," she explained. "It was my reason for coming home. The risk was too great for me to stay of course."

Toby grew silent the longer she talked and after a while, he quit working altogether. "You don't need to worry yourself about the notes, Tilly," he said softly, wiping his hands on his trousers. "You are perfectly safe."

"I don't think so," she argued. "You haven't read them, Toby! Mr Myers believes that I am a chaste, scandal free woman and if I ignore this, it could bring disgrace to not only me but him as well. I can't allow that." Brushing her own hands on her skirts, she shook her head. "Besides, I believe it is someone powerful, someone such as Lord Farthing. My father, he fought with him the night he died. I wouldn't put it past someone like Lord Farthing to stage his suicide and walk away." It had been on her mind for many years that she believed her father wouldn't leave her in such a manner. He had loved her. She often wondered if Lord Farthing had actually killed her father that evening, making it look like the captain had taken his own life instead to cover his tracks. There had been no witnesses and Aunt Ruth had never informed Tilly who had found the body.

Toby sighed. "You don't need to worry about Lord Farthing. He is not the one that has been writing the letters to you. Your aunt has."

For a moment, Tilly didn't think she had heard him correctly. Her aunt wouldn't do such a thing, frightening her own ward, and for what? To have her come back home? "No. It is not possible."

He stood up, his expression forlorn. "It is. Your aunt, she was also the one writing the letters to your father. She didn't approve of what he was doing to you, of the risk he was taking by incurring the debts on the household, and she wanted him to be frightened enough to stop. She wanted a good future for you, you see, and she knew that your father was going to force you both to the poorhouse before it was all over."

Tilly shot to her feet, her entire body trembling. It couldn't be possible. Her aunt loved her. She would never do something that would have caused her father's death, not her.

"She didn't know what lengths he would go to," Toby said softly, his eyes on the horizon. "She didn't anticipate that he would take his own life."

Tilly gasped, the hurt and anguish building up within her. It was horrid enough that she'd had to endure her father's death, but to know that her aunt had a hand in it. It was beyond comprehension. "I... I don't understand."

Toby's mouth tried to form the words. "We were in love, Tilly, though the captain didn't think that I was strong enough to support his sister-in-law from the beginning. Ruth, she couldn't leave you in such a state, not knowing if your father would be able to support you in the future and that you would likely end up in a bad way if she allowed him to continue doing what he was. She had hoped that the letters would make him stop, to think about you for once and not his need for cash." He looked at Tilly. "I didn't know until after we had moved and then not for the longest time."

Tilly couldn't breathe. She took a few steps away from Toby, her arm around her waist as she struggled to comprehend his words. Her aunt had caused her father's death. She had wanted him to take care of her but in turn, her plans had backfired, and Tilly had been left without a father completely.

"I know you feel anger toward her," Toby said in a soft voice. "But hear her out Tilly. She did it with you in mind."

Tilly whirled around, her eyes flashing. "It cost me my father! How could I possibly think that *she* did it with me in mind? She could have confronted him, threatened to take me away, something other than to cause me this, this pain and suffering, for years on end!"

Toby flinched but Tilly was already moving, heading out of the park at a clipped pace. She didn't care if her aunt was trying to rest now. She wanted to hear it from her mouth, to force her to say the words that Tilly thought she would never hear.

Fortunately, her aunt was back in the kitchen when Tilly entered the home, her expression worn. "Tilly," she said as she poured a cup of tea. "I wasn't expecting you today."

"Tell me it is not true," Tilly cried, her voice hard. "Tell me you didn't kill my father."

Her aunt's eyes widened, and she carefully set the teapot down on the table. "Tilly, I..."

"I want the truth," Tilly added, crossing her arms over her chest. "No more lies."

Her aunt's shoulders slumped. "I was worried that you were going down the same path as your father, that you would get hurt somehow, so I sent the letters to you, to bring you back."

Tilly tried to form the right words. "You took me from something I have enjoyed doing because you thought I would get hurt?"

"I admit," her aunt continued, her jaw clenching, "that it might not have been the right way to handle the situation, but you've been through so much."

"Because of you!" Tilly exclaimed, fighting back the tears. "My father..."

"I didn't mean for him to kill himself," her aunt interrupted. "He was so stubborn and no matter how many times I told him that he was going to end up in the poorhouse, he would find another way to prove me wrong. All your father did was pile on the debts that we already had and try to force you to become someone you weren't."

While that might have been true, it hadn't given Aunt Ruth the right to take matters into her own hands, not like that. "You should have told him that you were behind the letters."

Her aunt looked down at her hands. "I was planning on doing so the night that Lord Farthing showed up. It was clear that he knew you were a girl, and he was quite upset with your father about the people he had duped and lied to. It didn't bode well for Lord Farthing's reputation to be fooled so and he knew that if anyone found out, he would be a laughingstock."

Tilly felt the tears stream down her cheeks, she felt as if she was losing her father all over again. "You tried to control my life," she said raising her voice. "When I was a little girl and still now! Did you ever consider that I was happy at the flower shop, that I had found somewhere I belonged!"

Aunt Ruth had the grace to look embarrassed. "You are too headstrong for your own good, Matilda."

Tilly let out a guttural laugh. "But my life is mine, not yours. If I make a misstep, then I will have to work out how to make it right, myself." She pointed at her aunt, who had become ashen. "You have quite possibly lost me a future, aunt, a future that I would have flourished in. Do you know that I have been asked for my hand in marriage?"

The older woman's eyes widened once more but Tilly wasn't about to listen to another word that her aunt wanted to say, striding to the door angrily. "I am going to try and put right what you have done," she said, picking up her belongings. "And perhaps as I am doing so, I might find a way to forgive you one day."

"Matilda."

Tilly's shoulders stiffened but she forced herself to turn and meet her aunt's tortured gaze. "Know that everything I have done was for you," Aunt Ruth said softly, tears in her eyes. "I might not have done it the correct way, but I did it because I loved you. I still love you and I will love you until the end of my days. Nothing can ever change that."

Turning, Tilly opened the door and marched out, tears blinding her gaze. She had thought she was coming to a safe haven here today, but all she had learnt was that she had been lied to for years by the one person she thought she could trust.

As Tilly started down the pavement, back to the flower shop so that she could beg for her position back, she realised that her aunt wasn't a horrid person.

CHAPTER 13

Tilly found Mr Myers out the back of the shop, tending to the morning's delivery and the plants he had raised from seed. "So, you have returned," he murmured, his eyes on the seedlings.

Tilly placed her bag on the floor, suddenly weary from the recent turn of events. "I have and I would like a chance to explain."

Mr Myers brushed his hands on his apron. "Then, I would like to hear your explanation."

They sat down at the small table; Tilly clasping her hands together in her lap. "When I was younger," she started, finding the words difficult to say, "my father thought it a good idea to dress me as a boy and allow me to play chess in the drawing rooms of the

London elite. He made some immensely powerful friends and amassed funds in several ways, but he also accumulated a great deal of debt. I... I continued to hide behind my disguise, but one powerful gentleman found out and confronted my father. In turn, my father ended up taking his own life." She decided to leave out her aunt's role in her father's death, her heart still too tender to discuss the betrayal. "I moved to London with my aunt, then recently I've been receiving threats about my past."

Mr Myers drew in a sharp breath, his small round eyes growing angered.

"I didn't want to bring any scandal to you or your shop," she rushed on. "You saw me as someone who was unattached from scandal, and I would have been a good person to carry on your legacy, but I am not, and I couldn't take on that role." There, she had said it. She wasn't the perfect person he thought she was, nor the right one to be his successor, no matter how much it pained her to admit.

Mr Myers let out a slow breath, looking down at his own worn, scarred hands. "Why didn't you come and tell me as soon as you received the first note?"

"Because I didn't think it was something to be concerned about," Tilly admitted, her cheeks flushing. "But when the others started to come, I knew I had to leave." She felt as if it had been the right thing to do, though if she had known that her aunt was behind it the entire time, she wouldn't have given up so quickly.

"I could have helped you," Mr Myers said after a moment. "I could have alerted the authorities and provided protection." He eyed her. "Is there still a threat?"

Tilly shook her head. "I found out who was the one sending the missives. They will no longer be doing so."

"Are you certain?"

"Yes," she answered softly and with great pain in her heart. She didn't know how she was ever going to forgive her aunt for what she had done, but Tilly knew she would eventually. Above all, she was her only remaining relative and both the twins were ignorant to what their mother had been doing. She still wished to know them.

Mr Myers placed his hands on the table, pushing himself out of the chair slowly. "Then we have nothing further to discuss."

Tilly's heart cracked open, and she stood quietly. "I understand."

He looked back, arching a grey brow. "Do you now, girl?"

"You're asking me to leave."

Mr Myers chuckled, shaking his head. "No, I'm not. Do you not realise how much I would have preferred you to have been truthful with me than to feel as if you had to hide your problems? We all have problems, Tilly, problems that run deep. What is important is that we understand those issues and overcome them to make us a better person."

Tilly drew in a painful breath, perilously close to tears once more. He didn't see her as anything other than the person she had been in the beginning. "You aren't going to let me go?" she asked, hopeful that she had heard him correctly.

"No, I'm not," he replied. "And if you are still interested in taking over the shop, I would be honoured to have you become the owner and proprietor one day."

Tears did fall from Tilly's eyes then. "Truly?" She hadn't ruined everything after all! "I... I would be honoured to do so."

"Then it's settled," he stated, nodding to her apron that was still hanging on the nail nearby. "Now, let's get to work."

Tilly smiled and did as he asked, working throughout the remainder of the day. All the worries of her past, of what her aunt had done, slid off her shoulders as she created lovely arrangements, bouquets and displays that would be put in the shop window for sale the next day, incorporating some of her favourite flowers as a sign of a new future.

Dusk was settling by the time they closed the shop and Mr Myers stripped off his apron. "I am off now to join Orla for dinner," he announced as his daughter came down the stairs. Tilly was surprised to see Orla transformed from a giggly teenager to a lovely young woman, dressed in a dark emerald-green gown that matched her eyes perfectly. "You look lovely," Tilly stated as Orla joined them.

Orla flushed as she fidgeted with her reticule. "We are going to dinner with a suitor."

"That's wonderful," Tilly said truthfully, glad that the young woman had found someone as well.

Mr Myers took his hat from his daughter, glancing over toward Tilly. "And your suitor?"

Tilly managed a smile. "I will be looking for him shortly." She needed to tell Emrys all of what had happened today with her aunt and to give him the answer to his question he has asked her earlier.

The older man chuckled as he opened the door, allowing his daughter to go through first. "I don't think you'll have to look far, Tilly."

Puzzled, Tilly followed the two of them out and found Emrys leaning up against the wall, his hands shoved in his pockets with a lazy grin on his face. "There you are," he murmured, pushing away from the wall.

"As if you couldn't see me through the window," Tilly countered, feeling suddenly nervous. She had no need to be but in the few hours she had been back at the shop, their kiss had filtered through her mind more than once.

"Ah, I could indeed," Emrys replied as he took her hands, warming them in his own, "but it is nothing like seeing you in person, my love."

Tilly's heart melted and she moved toward him, until he was encircling her in his strong arms. "How is it that you are back here?" he asked, his lips above her ear.

His scent surrounded her, and Tilly sighed as she pressed her cheek to the coarse material of his shirt. "My aunt was behind the notes."

Emrys pulled her back abruptly and tucked her arm into his, setting them on the path toward a well-lit area of town. "This demands a brisk walk while you explain everything to me."

Tilly did just that and by the time they reached the very park she had denied his first proposal, Emrys was cursing under his breath. "That, that wretched woman!"

"It does not matter," Tilly heard herself say. "She can't undo anything she has done, and my father, well, he's been dead for years. All I can do is move past it, though it will take some time for me to do so."

Emrys blew out a breath, his expression unchanged. "Well, then it seems that you have told Mr Myers about your sordid past?"

Tilly laughed, finding it quite easy to do so now that everything was out in the open. She had told those who meant something to her, like Mr Myers and Emrys, and that would be all who needed to know.

Just as she was about to tell Emrys what he wished to hear from her, another figure came upon them. "There you are!"

Startled, Tilly turned to find Lord Farthing standing there, his hat in his hands. His face was more wrinkled than she remembered, but it had been ten years since she had last seen him, so it was to be expected. "You are Wainwright's daughter, are you not?"

Emrys drew close to Tilly's side, and she was grateful that he was there. "I am," Tilly said, straightening her shoulders. She wasn't going to hide any longer, not even from someone who might wish to do her harm. She was Captain George Wainwright's daughter, and nothing could change that.

Lord Farthing cleared his throat. "I know that your father's death was hard on you, but I am glad to see that you have become a lovely young woman." His expression grew sorrowful. "I've always regretted the last conversation I had with the captain. I was very upset that he had lied to me about your actual identity, and I lashed out at him in the wrong way."

Tilly was surprised and shocked that the gentleman was saying those words to her. Emrys's arm slid around her waist, and she allowed herself to lean into his muscular body. "I don't know what to say."

"You don't have to say anything," Lord Farthing replied softly. "But if you ever need anything at all, Miss Wainwright, please reach out. I will consider it an honour to carry on your father's legacy."

"Thank you," she said, meaning it. "I'm afraid I thought the worst when I heard you and father fight that evening."

"I should have never let my anger get away from me," Lord Farthing added, regret clear as day in his expression. "Your father, well, he had his own problems, but who does not? I was upset that he hadn't trusted me enough to tell me the truth and, when I found out, I was hurt and felt betrayed."

Tilly could understand. She had felt the same about her father and her aunt, how they both, in their own way, had betrayed her.

"I must be getting on," Lord Farthing stated after a few awkward moments. "But I would like to have you over for dinner sometime, Matilda."

"I would like that too," Tilly answered. Perhaps in learning more about the gentleman, her heart could start to heal.

The gentleman turned and walked away, leaving Tilly dumbfounded. What had started out as a horrid day had turned into something special, something she really hadn't expected.

"Well," Emrys said, turning Tilly towards him. "That was most unexpected."

"Completely," she added. "But it is nice to know that someone such as him is happy to associate with me."

Emrys chuckled, his eyes flickering with laughter. "So, Matilda Wainwright, do you have an answer to my question or are you going to allow me to suffer yet another day of loneliness?"

Tilly shook her head, a smile playing on her lips. "I doubt you are ever lonely."

"I have been since the moment I met you and had to walk away every single time," Emrys replied gently, brushing her cheek with his hand. "I would rather not ever walk away from you again, Tilly."

Tilly leaned into his touch. "I would like that too, Emrys."

His eyes widened, as if he were surprised at her answer. "Truly?"

"I would love to marry you and become your wife," she answered, pressing her lips to his cheek. "That is if you are still proposing marriage?"

Emrys pulled away and stared into her eyes, showing Tilly the tenderness that she had felt in his words, his touch now reflected in his gaze. "I would be thrilled," he said, his voice hoarse. "For you to be my wife."

"Then I would be honoured," she replied, tears glistening in her eyes. They embraced and some of the anger, regret, and remorse slid away from Tilly's heart. Emrys was her future now.

"Even if you will beat me soundly at chess," he murmured, lifting his head to gaze into her eyes.

"And can arrange flowers better than I could ever dream of doing."

Tilly pursed her lips, a bubble of laughter nearly escaping. "I suppose I could take it easy on you from time to time," she offered, reaching up to brush his cheek gently with her fingertips.

He captured them and brought them to his mouth, pressing a kiss on each one of the tips. "Never do such a thing. I can take all that you give me and more."

She believed him and when he captured her lips with his, Tilly knew that she had found her home, a place where her heart would reside forever.

EPILOGUE

ONE YEAR LATER...

*T*illy gazed at herself in the mirror, adjusting the lacy veil around her shoulders. After a one-year engagement, the day had come for her and Emrys to wed. The day had been a little while coming but a great deal had happened in the year since the night that Emrys had proposed to her.

Drawing in a breath, Tilly picked up the bouquet of flowers that she had arranged a few days before, inhaling the sweet scent to calm her nerves. Tucked deep inside the bouquet was the small iron flower that Emrys had given her, and Tilly couldn't help but smile at the memory. Now they would have many more memories to cherish between them.

Now she was making a lifetime of memories. The flower shop was hers now and she had been hard at work to make minor changes to attract even more clientele. One of the most exciting things that had happened was that she had gained a royal warrant and her arrangements were gracing various rooms that the Royal Family frequented. It had raised her profile, increasing her funds, which had allowed Tilly to purchase a small greenhouse to keep some of the plants she was cultivating by hand in.

That wasn't all that had happened. Mr Myers was now living with Orla and her new husband, having wed six months earlier and she was already expecting their first child. She and Orla had become closer, and Tilly made certain to visit Orla and her father once a week to give them updates on the shop and any gossip that she had heard. Tilly could scarcely believe that this was her livelihood now, but when she awoke each morning, she felt a sense of rightness within herself.

To preserve her reputation, Tilly had hired another woman, Julia, to help in the shop. Julia was the daughter of a well to do family, but she too had a strong desire to be her own woman, instead of simply marrying a wealthy gentleman. They had met by chance as Julia longingly gazed at Tilly's window display and scarcely two weeks later, Julia was moving in. They had become lasting friends with Julia having good connections and ideas on how to approach the gentry.

With Emrys's urging, Tilly had also approached Lord Farthing for another favour, after having heard about a London Chess club that catered to gentlemen only. While Tilly would have been content to just focus on her floral talents, her fiancée had pushed her to chase after all her dreams. Tilly still remembered the day that she had called upon the London gentleman, how she had marvelled still over his opulent home as she was shown to his sitting room.

He had greeted her warmly, which was a pleasant surprise to Tilly herself, and after informing him that she wanted to join the club, he had decided that she was a perfect candidate.

All she needed was a sponsor and over the next few days, Tilly and Lord Farthing went from home to home, showing off her skills with the chess set and gathering a growing number of titled women that would influence their husbands to put their support behind Tilly.

The first night she had stepped over the threshold of the chess club, Tilly had been horribly nervous. Lord Farthing had accompanied her and after giving her words of encouragement, she had soundly beaten some of the more skilled players of the club, solidifying her spot in what had been a gentleman's only club before then. Since her eventual acceptance, three more women had come to the club and proven their worth as far as their own skills and now Tilly had a small, close circle of friends that shared the same passion as she did.

Her love for Emrys had been more than she could have ever wanted. He was still a Leerie, though he had been taking lessons from Mr Myers as to how to help her run the business, and even Lord Farthing on what it meant to become a proper gentleman. Every time they were able to spend some time alone, he regaled her with his lessons and while Tilly would never want him to do anything that made him unhappy, Emrys seemed to thrive on the attention.

She couldn't care less what he did as long as he was with her.

A happy sigh escaped her as a knock sounded on the door and it opened to reveal a dapper looking Toby. "Are you ready?" he asked, his eyes taking in her simple cream-coloured gown. "You are quite lovely, Tilly."

She flushed. "Thank you, Toby, and yes, I'm ready."

He arched a brow. "You could still run you know. There's a carriage out front."

Tilly laughed and shook her head. "No, I don't wish to leave Emrys behind."

Toby proffered his arm. "Then let's get you wed."

Tilly began her walk down the aisle and got her first glimpse of the full church waiting on her. Her gaze wandered over her friends from the chess club, men and women alike, seated in the pews decorated with her favourite flowers, giving her nods and smiles as she passed. Tilly also found Mr Myers, Orla, and her husband Christopher near the front, Orla dabbing her eyes and giving Tilly a little wave. Lord Farthing and his wife were also there, dressed in wedding finery and Tilly was glad that he was there. He had become a close friend to her and Emrys over the past year.

The last person Tilly sought out was her Aunt Ruth, seated in the front row with her two nephews dressed in their Sunday best next to her. They locked eyes and Tilly gave her a small nod, letting her know that she was grateful that her aunt had decided to come after all. Their relationship was slowly repairing itself and while the hurt still felt fresh in her heart, Tilly had finally let go of any hatred she had felt for what her aunt had done. Truly, it wasn't her fault that the captain had decided to take his own life, but the hurt was going to be there for some time to come.

Finally, she reached a waiting Emrys, whose eyes misted over when he saw Tilly in her gown. Tilly's own throat grew tight as she took in his suit, how handsome he looked waiting on her.

He was about to become her husband and Tilly couldn't wait any longer. She loved him fiercely. "It is about time you got here," he murmured cheekily as he took her hand from Toby with a nod. "I don't like that they are all staring at me as if I'm expected to perform tricks."

Tilly attempted and failed to smother a light giggle, which had the vicar looking at them disapprovingly. "I do apologise," she said immediately, smiling as Emrys winked at her. It was certainly not going to be a boring rest of her days, not with him by her side.

When it came time to say their vows, Tilly said them loud and clear, feeling the emotion well up within her as she repeated the words and watched as Emrys slipped the simple gold band on her ring finger. "You may now kiss the bride," the vicar announced, stepping back. Emrys stepped closer and Tilly smiled at him as he cupped her cheek, brushing his lips over hers. "After waiting for so long," he stated softly, so as no one else could hear him, "you are finally mine."

"And you are mine," she informed him before they turned to the smiling guests.

They were at last a wedded couple.

Grinning, Tilly met the eyes of those that she cared for, including the tear-stained cheeks of her aunt. All was going to be well in her life from this moment forward. She could feel it in her bones. "Come, my fair Mrs. Thomas," Emrys murmured, saying her new wedded name. "Shall we head out to our lovely wedding feast?"

Tilly looked at her husband, her cheeks pink with excitement. "We shall, my handsome Mr Thomas."

Emrys brought their joined hands to his lips, brushing his lips over her knuckles. "Then let's set off into the rest of our lives together."

A few months later...

TILLY SWITCHED the sign to closed and locked the door tightly, turning the lamps off as she passed. The weather was turning colder, and the drafts never seemed to end, no matter how warm they kept the shop and their small home upstairs.

This evening, however, Tilly didn't make her way up the stairs but rather behind them, where two comfortable chairs were set up before the warm fireplace. Between the chairs was her beloved chess set, the pieces well-worn from the many games they had experienced together. In the few months that they had been wed, Tilly hadn't thought that she could be happier than she was, but each day brought something new and exciting to their marriage. She was constantly learning more about Emrys, about his likes and dislikes. There had been little adjustment with them living together and now she couldn't imagine her life without him in it every single day.

Much like Toby and her aunt.

There was more, however. She was flourishing at the chess club and recently had been asked to participate in a large tournament that would bring players from other countries, including the one Frenchmen that her father had wanted her to play all those years ago. This time it would not be for any monetary gain, but Tilly was still excited by the prospect.

Emrys's red head was peeking out from over the top of the chair and Tilly's heart softened as she rounded the seat. "Is everything all right?" he asked softly as she joined him, sitting in her chair. His eyes were alight with tenderness as Tilly nodded. "Everything is fine," she answered with a smile, her eyes flickering to the chess board. "Are you sure you are prepared tonight?"

Her husband chuckled, his long fingers touching one of the pawns. "I am always prepared, my love. The problem is you get better each time we play."

Tilly grinned. She had learned a few new moves herself from the chess club members and enjoyed trying them out on Emrys, much to his chagrin.

Emrys had got better with his play, but he had yet to beat her, preferring that she not take it easy on him.

"Perhaps you will find some luck one of these days."

Emrys snorted. "I doubt it, but I love you regardless. You can beat me in the quiet of our home as many times as you wish, Tilly."

Tilly smiled and moved her first pawn. The game was afoot…

~*~*~

Thank you so much for reading my story.

If you enjoyed reading this book may I suggest that you might also like to read my recent release 'Saving the Wretched Slum Girl' next which is available on Amazon for just £0.99 or free with Kindle Unlimited.

Click Here to Get Your Copy Today!

∾

Sample of First Chapter

Seven-year-old Alice Smythe was small for her age, which in some ways was a bonus as it allowed her to work as a scavenger mule at the Langford Cotton Mill, in the East End of London. She and her mother had worked there together for the past six months, Alice having commenced her employment at the mill the day after her seventh birthday.

They toiled from dawn till dusk often not seeing the outside light during the day at all. She listened intently to the clacking of the machinery as it moved back and forth, the spindle catching the yarn at the top and winding it up, as if it were a spinning top she had seen once at the travelling fair.

Alice needed to be careful when she scrambled underneath, she knew the work was dangerous—her mother had reminded her many times—but her family needed the money to survive. The loud deafening sound of the busy machinery no longer hurt her ears as it had in her first few months, her mother had told her to push some cotton fluff in them to dull the noise and she wore a remnant of cloth across her mouth to keep the loose threads and cotton dust from clogging up her throat and lungs.

Her mother suffered from a nasty cough, brought on by years of working in the hot, humid conditions that were needed in a cotton mill. She would hear her in the middle of the night getting up gasping for air, drinking to try and relieve the spasms, but nothing seemed to help. Her cough was getting much worse but still she needed to work else they would end up in the workhouse and that would be dishonourable beyond words. No one ever wanted to end up there, it would be a disgrace.

As quick as a mouse, she darted under the dangerous mechanical movement, keeping her head low, almost touching the filthy wooden floor as she gathered up the loose cotton balls that had fallen from the equipment. Her small nimble fingers tucked them into the pocket of the dark apron that her mother had placed around her waist just this morning. Dashing forward before the machine could complete another turn, Alice darted out on the other side—she was safe this time.

Even at the young age of seven, Alice knew that there was a heavy risk around the machines. Her mother would warn her several times a day to be careful about watching her head and keeping her wits about her at all times. While she didn't enjoy the task she had been given, Alice knew that her family badly needed the extra money now that her father wasn't able to work. It was up to Alice and her mother, Mary to find the necessary finances to support them. They were luckier than some, she was an only child, Alice couldn't imagine how hard it must be for families with several children.

Alice hurried around the machine, placing the loose cotton scraps into the storage barrel that would be taken away at the end of the day, dumping the oddments into the large vats of leftover fragments. Alice liked the way the soft cotton felt between her fingertips. Just the other day she had put some in her pocket and taken it home, keeping it under her pillow to touch in the cold dark nights. She would have been whipped by Master Turney, the foreman, if he had found out, but Alice hadn't been forced to empty her pockets that particular day, so no one knew and now she had something of her own that no one else knew about.

Not even her mother…

"Alice! Stop daydreaming. The cotton isn't going to pick itself up!"

Her mother's voice cut through her thoughts and Alice darted under the machine once more, gathering up the cotton. A few strands of fine blonde hair clung to Alice's moist neck as she quickly finished her task. Her mother made her wear a dark brown mop cap so that her hair wouldn't get trapped in the constantly moving machinery above her head, telling her daughter that she had seen it happen once, that a little girl had been scalped before they could stop the machines. All of Alice's clothes were either brown or black in colour, her mother insisted that she wear dark clothing. After all, you couldn't see the dirt if it was the same colour as the material, she would say.

"Smythe!"

Alice cringed at the sound of Master Turney's shrill voice, scurrying out of his path as he bared down on her mother. Having worked at the Langford Cotton Mill for most of her life, her mother didn't even flinch at the man's putrid breath hovering over her. "Yes, Master Turney?" she answered plainly.

He pointed at Alice, who was peeking out from behind one of the machines. "Why isn't your gel sweeping the floor like she is paid to do?" the man growled angrily.

"I will have her do it straightaway, Master Turney," her mother replied. Alice didn't waste any time finding the broom. Hurrying as far away as possible from the conversation, she set to sweeping up the dust and cotton fragments too small to be picked up. She didn't like Master Turney and very few workers at the factory did. He was a nasty vicious bully, who wouldn't think twice about using his fists to get what he wanted.

Her small body moved the broom furiously over the grimy floor, causing a small cloud of dust to rise which tickled her nose through her face covering, but she managed not to sneeze. In the near distance, she saw a familiar face, nine-year-old John Cartwright, walking through the hallway. It was unbelievable that he was back at work so soon after his terrible accident.

He was one of the piecers, a job known to be very dangerous, and John had proved the point. He had not been in work for the past few days. Alice remembered back to the day when John had been hurt, she had never seen so much blood before in her young life and, despite the fact that her mother had tried to shield her from it, Alice had still seen enough of the carnage to scare her for a lifetime.

Poor John had got his hand caught trying to repair the broken threads, he had foolishly tried to grab his cap that had been dislodged because he was growing too tall.

"What's he doin' here, he canna work like that?" the foreman shouted above the roar of the machines. "Look at that bandage, there's still blood seeping through."

"I promise ye he can still work, just as well. He's a strong lad. Put him on moving the barrels or helping with sweeping the floors. Please, I beg of ye," his mother, Myrtle pleaded. She was a thin scraggy woman and most folks in the factory knew that John and Myrtle depended on the work to support his younger siblings. His father had passed just five months ago from the same cough that Alice's poor mother was displaying.

Alice swallowed as her eyes trailed towards the bandage, gasping when she realised that it was evident that two of his fingers were not where they should be.

Shaking his head, Turney relented, sending John to the docking area where the cotton came in to be sent to the looms, yelling for the trembling woman to get back to her work too. The rest of the day passed by slowly and without incident and by the time the sun was starting to fade through the filth ingrained windows, Alice's hands were covered in fresh bulging blisters from holding the broom far too tightly.

Passing down the last aisle, she swept the dust away from the pathways between the looms. Just as she was finishing up, she heard raised voices and crept a little closer to the sound.

"I don't care what you were doing! You weren't here, Nicholas! That is all that matters. I want you here and in *my* bed at night."

"Now, you listen to me, I had business to attend to, Catherine. You couldn't possibly understand what I was doing."

Alice took a quick peek in the direction the voices were coming from, her eyes widening, when she saw the owner of the Mill, Mr Nicholas Langford, standing close by, next to his wife, Catherine Langford. Mr Langford was dressed in a fine dark charcoal grey suit, the shiny golden chain of a pocket watch swaying across the front of his rather portly stomach that was covered by colourful floral waistcoat. Catherine Langford was dressed in a gown that was perhaps the loveliest that Alice had ever seen, having a deep crimson colour with pretty cream coloured lacework at the neck and cuffs. Alice wondered if the material felt as soft and smooth as it looked.

She would never attempt to touch the fabric, however, that would never do, it would be cause for instant dismissal. She could see that Catherine Langford was annoyed as she glared angrily at her husband. Alice had seen that stance many times before. It was the same one that her mother liked to use when Alice was misbehaving. She was intrigued to know what was going on and she couldn't help but stand stock still and gawp as the couple continued to argue.

"Oh, Nicholas, I'm well aware of what you were doing," Catherine Langford said, her hands flying about wildly. "You were with that hussy again, weren't you?"

Mr Langford stepped forward, hands raised as he tried to placate his angry wife. "Come, come, you don't know what you are talking about."

Catherine Langford laughed audibly and there was a bitterness to the high-pitched sound. "Oh, Nicholas, I am not as naïve as you may think. I know you have a mistress and have done for some time." Alice gasped at the woman's strange words. She knew she shouldn't continue to listen to another's private conversation, but she simply couldn't help herself. Catherine Langford continued speaking, her voice a little lower now. "That is not why I sought you out though. Our son, Matthew, is due to return from school for the summer break. I expect he will be going back at the start of the autumn term."

"Mm-hm," Nicholas acknowledged, clearing his throat. "I'm not sure that is a good idea. I suggest he comes to work in the mill so he can come to understand some of what he is destined to inherit. It's about time he learnt the family trade. That's how I learnt the goings on of this establishment—from my father, not by spending money on an expensive education."

"I understand, but he will still be returning to school to finish his education. I insist," Mrs Langford stated plainly, pushing her index finger into the man's chest to prove her point. "He's destined for greatness. He may not have a title, but that does not matter in this time of vast economic growth."

"As you well know, my darling," the man replied, a cruel sneer spreading across his face. "This is our livelihood. It is what pays for your fancy gowns and afternoon teas with those simpering women you call your friends. Of course, he will finish the necessary education but then he is expected to learn how to run this factory. Too much of a fancy education isn't going to help without the practical experience to help him get on in life."

Catherine Langford didn't look as if she was about to back down and Alice waited to see what the man would do next. "As long as you allow him to complete his studies, I will be satisfied," she said placing her hands firmly on her hips. "But you are not to renege on your word."

"S'cuse me, Mr Langford. We need to talk about them workers and which ones ain't pulling their weight and what we need to do about 'em?"

The couple turned as Master Turney approached them, causing Alice to shrink back into the shadows, her young mind attempting to sort out the conversation she had just overheard. So, the owner had a son, one that she was not aware of. What good fortune he had, never needing to work in this grimy, dirt-laden mill but going to school to learn to read and write, something she had always dreamt of doing.

Sighing with frustration, she quickly finished her work before making her way back to her mother. "Ready, my darling gel?" her mother asked trying to smother a cough, tightening the scarf around her head and handing Alice her coat. "There is a cold wind out there. We wouldn't want to catch our deaths, so button up and come along with me," she continued holding out her hand for Alice to take.

Alice donned her coat and thin woollen scarf before making their way down the stone steps with the other workers, their workday finally at an end. Alice stayed close to her mother as they exited the mill, grasping her hand lightly. The lamp lighters were already out, lighting the smoggy streets, allowing them a dull glow with which to find their way home. By the time they got back, Alice's nose was red and streaming from the cold.

Her father eagerly awaited them inside, leaning heavily on his crutch as they entered in a flurry. "There you are," he cried as Alice shrugged out of her coat. "I have made us some dinner."

Her mother gave him a grateful smile, knowing that there was little food to be had and it would have been difficult to cook something nourishing for them all. "That was kind of you, Frank. I'm sorry we are late."

Alice gave her father a tight hug, careful not to topple him over. "Thank you, Papa."

"Oh, my darling gel. You don't have to thank me for anything," he said, returning her embrace.

Alice gazed up at him and saw the sadness in his eyes as he looked down at her. Her father had also once worked in the mill. However, an inexperienced hand had incorrectly stacked some barrels, causing them to escape their confines, crushing his leg beyond repair. With his badly deformed leg and the crutch he required to get around, no mill was willing to offer him work—to them he was as good as useless.

It didn't matter to Alice, though, he was still her Papa and she loved him more than anybody else in the world, apart from her Mama of course, who she loved equally.

"Come, Alice," her mother said pulling her towards the enamel washbasin. "Let's get cleaned up."

Alice dutifully did as her mother asked, forcing her hands into the frigid water.

Her stomach grumbled, reminding her of how hungry she was, although there would be barely enough food, being that the family had to survive on the pittance that she and her mother earned. Times may be hard in the Smythe household, but Alice knew there was always plenty of love to go around.

~*~*~

This wonderful Victorian Romance story — 'Saving the Wretched Slum Girl' — is available on Amazon for just £0.99 or *FREE* with Kindle Unlimited simply by clicking on the link below.

Click Here to Get Your Copy of 'Saving the Wretched Slum Girl' - Today!

A NOTE FROM THE AUTHOR

Dear Reader,

Thank you so much for choosing and reading my story — I sincerely hope it lived up to your expectations and that you enjoyed it as much as I loved writing about the Victorian era.

This age was a time of great industrial expansion with new inventions and advancements.

However, it is true to say that there was a distinct disparity amongst the population at that time — one that I like to emphasise, allowing the characters in my stories to have the chance to grow and change their lives for the better.

Best Wishes
Ella Cornish

Newsletter

If you love reading Victorian Romance stories…

**Simply sign up here and get your FREE copy of
The Orphan's Despair**

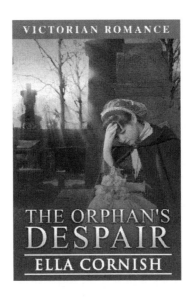

Click Here to Download Your Copy - Today!

More Stories from Ella!

If you enjoyed reading this story you can find more great reads from Ella on Amazon...

Click Here for More Stories from Ella Cornish

Contact Me

If you'd simply like to drop us a line you can contact us at **ellacornishauthor@gmail.com**

You can also connect with me on my Facebook Page **https://www.facebook.com/ellacornishauthor/**

I will always let you know about new releases on my Facebook page, so it is worth liking that if you get the chance.

LIKE Ella's Facebook Page **_HERE_**

I welcome your thoughts and would love to hear from you!

Printed in Great Britain
by Amazon

10006519R20111